D0191880

SECRETS
OF
SHAKESPEARE'S
GRAVE

NO LONGER PROPERTY OF
SEATTLE PUBLIC LIBRARY

Letterford

Received On:

DEC 16 2015

Fremont Library

SECRETS

OF

SHAKESPEARE'S

GRAVE

BY DERON R. HICKS

ILLUSTRATED BY MARK EDWARD GEYER

HOUGHTON MIFFLIN HARCOURT
BOSTON NEW YORK

Copyright © 2012 by Deron R. Hicks
Illustrations copyright © 2012 by Mark Edward Geyer

All rights reserved. Originally published in hardcover in the United States by
Houghton Mifflin Books for Children, an imprint of Houghton Mifflin Harcourt
Publishing Company, 2012.
For information about permission to reproduce selections from this book, write to
Permissions, Houghton Mifflin Harcourt Publishing Company, 215 Park Avenue
South, New York, New York 10003.

www.hmhco.com

The text of this book is set in New Century Schoolbook.
The illustrations are pen and ink.
Book design by Carol Chu

The Library of Congress has cataloged the hardcover edition as follows:
Hicks, Deron R.
Secrets of Shakespeare's grave / by Deron R. Hicks ;
[illustrated by Mark Edward Geyer].
p. cm.
Summary: "Twelve-year-old Colophon Letterford has a serious mystery on
her hands. Will she discover the link between her family's literary legacy and
Shakespeare's tomb before it's too late?" —Provided by publisher.
[1. Mystery and detective stories. 2. Adventure and adventurers—Fiction.
3. Family-owned business enterprises—Fiction. 4. Brothers and sisters—Fiction.
5. Cousins—Fiction.] I. Geyer, Mark, ill. II. Title.
PZ7.H531615Sec 2012
[Fic]—dc23
2012014801

ISBN 978-0-547-84034-5 hardcover
ISBN 978-0-544-10504-1 paperback

Manufactured in the U.S.A.
DOC 10 9 8 7 6
4500518833

FOR
ANGELA,
MEG,
✦
PARKER

Contents

Prologue

Le Mont Saint-Michel
May 1, 1616

Wind, rain, and waves have pounded the rocky coast of Normandy for thousands of years. The forces of nature slowly eroded the vast coastal plains to form a large bay and, in the middle of that bay — apparently oblivious to the onslaught of nature—remained an impossibly large granite rock. According to legend, the archangel Michael appeared to the bishop of Avranches in A.D. 708 and demanded the construction of a church on that rock. The bishop, who apparently had other items on his agenda, ignored the archangel's demands. The archangel, however, would not be deterred. With a touch of his finger, the archangel burned a hole in the bishop's skull.

The bishop got the message.

The church was built.

To honor the legend of Archangel Michael, the rock has been known for centuries as Saint Michael's Mountain—or more commonly, le Mont Saint-Michel. At the highest peak of le Mont Saint-Michel stands the abbey church, hewn from the native granite and surrounded by beautiful gardens maintained by the Benedictine monks who have lived in the adjacent cloister for centuries. A narrow stone road winds its way up the rock, and through a small village that sits below the church. The church, the cloister, and the village are surrounded by a fortified wall—a testament to the rock's history as a token of war. However, it is the raging tides of the bay that surround and truly protect le Mont Saint-Michel. The tides are not timid—they are said to be the swiftest and deepest in Europe. Many a man has lost his life for failing to pay due respect to the charging waters.

Over the centuries le Mont Saint-Michel had served as a fortress, a prison, and a sanctuary. On this particular evening, however, Miles Letterford hoped that it would offer both a brief respite from his long trek and the answer to his quest. He had set out from England five days prior, but the weather had not been cooperative. On many occasions he had been sorely tempted to turn back from this arduous and unusual journey. Just a week ago he had been sitting by the bed of his dying friend. His friend had placed a ring in the palm of his hand and asked him to swear an oath—an oath to recover and keep safe that which his friend treasured most. Miles now silently cursed his rashness in agreeing to such an undertaking.

The relentless weather of the Norman coast had left him cold, wet, and exhausted as he arrived at the edge of the bay at dusk. In front of him was le Mont Saint-Michel. The massive rock—its village lights flickering in the distance—seemed to float on the low fog that covered the bay. Miles could see the silhouette of the abbey church at the top of le Mont.

His arrival coincided with low tide, and he knew that the sea had retreated far beyond the imposing rock. This was not, as he had been warned, a guarantee of safe passage, and the fading light and fog made the situation particularly dangerous—the bay was not a place to dally. Miles spurred his horse on toward the glittering lights of le Mont.

The ride across the bay took far longer than Miles had anticipated. The lights—so clear from the far shore—were rendered almost nonexistent by the thick fog that now enveloped him and his horse. Miles wondered more than once whether he had rambled off course—whether he would eventually run into the teeth of the returning tide. He was therefore greatly relieved when the light from a lamp outside the village gates finally burned its way through the thick haze and offered him a guidepost.

Once inside the village gates, Miles found a public stable where, for a small fee, his weary horse was permitted some hay and shelter from the weather. Although his body ached and his stomach protested, he knew that he would have to wait for his food and rest.

The rain had now passed and night had come; the sky opened to reveal a full moon. Miles walked quickly through the empty, moonlit streets of the village, up a steep set of stone stairs, and onto a landing at the top of le Mont. The imposing stone facade of the abbey church now towered above him, its spire reaching far into the night sky.

Miles looked around the landing.

He was alone.

He opened the heavy wooden door of the church and slipped quietly inside.

He stood inside the entrance and stared down the nave. The church was dimly lit—four small lanterns offered only the merest hint of the space within. Looking upward offered nothing more—whatever moonlight illuminated le Mont could not penetrate windows darkened by centuries of candle soot. He could not see the ceiling—just darkness. The shadows in the side aisles hung like curtains. Everything was black and gray.

Miles stepped into the shadows of the side aisle and listened intently.

He heard nothing.

The monks who inhabited the abbey followed a rigid schedule—a schedule that called for them to be in their rooms for evening prayers for at least the next hour. The church itself was used only for mass in the morning and vespers in the evening. Otherwise it remained empty, except for the occasional pilgrim and cleaning—neither of which would be expected at this time of night.

Satisfied that he was alone, Miles walked down the nave to the center of the church—the crossing—and turned right down a short passage. At the end of the passage, several small prayer candles burned on a wooden pedestal. Above him towered a large wooden sculpture of Archangel Michael, standing triumphantly with his right arm raised high above his head, a flaming sword in his hand, and under his left foot, the decapitated head of a dragon.

Miles pulled out his dagger, paused, and listened once again.

Nothing.

He placed his left hand on the top edge of the pedestal and felt along its edge. Almost two-thirds down the edge, he found what he was looking for—a small, almost imperceptible notch. He placed the tip of his dagger in the notch and pulled.

CRACK

The sound reverberated through the church. The front of the pedestal separated slightly from the rest of the base.

Miles listened for any sounds.

Again, nothing.

Miles set the dagger in the crack in the pedestal and pulled again.

The wood groaned and then . . . CRACK. The front of the pedestal separated a full hand's width from the base.

Miles paused and listened once again.

Nothing.

He grabbed the front of the pedestal, took a deep breath, and pulled.

CRACK

The front of the pedestal had now separated entirely from the rest of the base. Miles carefully placed the front of the pedestal aside, grabbed one of the pilgrim candles, and held it up to the base. The base, as he expected, was hollow. Inside was a box, which he carefully removed.

Miles examined the box. It was constructed of dark, almost black wood, edged at its corners with inlaid brass. Carved into the top of the box was a falcon holding a spear with the words *non sanz droict* inscribed beneath. On the front of the box was a large brass oval inscribed with the symbol for the Greek letter sigma—Σ.

Miles ran his hand over the carving on the top of the box. It was exactly as described to him. His heart raced with anticipation, the long and demanding journey now forgotten.

In his excitement, however, Miles did not hear the footsteps behind him.

WHACK

The first blow went directly into his ribs.

WHACK

The second blow struck him below his right shoulder blade.

Miles dropped the box and tumbled to his side in pain. He gasped for air as he looked up and saw standing above him a large bald man dressed in a gray tunic—the traditional vestments of a Benedictine monk. In his hand he held a thick wooden staff. His face was red with rage.

"Thief!" the monk growled. "Wretched vile miscreant!"

Miles attempted to scramble to his feet, but another blow to his back sent him flat to the ground.

"Ill-bred, beef-witted varlet!" the monk hissed.

Miles struggled to catch his breath. His chest burned. "Wait . . . ," he coughed.

"Fie upon you!" the monk exclaimed. "Ye will get no sympathy from me!"

Miles crawled toward the crossing as the beating continued.

WHACK

"Villain!"

WHACK

"Louse!"

WHACK

"Venomous cutpurse!"

Miles reached the crossing and rolled over onto his back. The monk—sweat pouring from his bald head—stood over him and raised his staff high, ready to strike. Miles covered his face with his hands and awaited the next blow.

But the next blow never came.

Miles waited, eyes closed, hands over his face.

Nothing.

He chanced a peek at his attacker. To his surprise, the monk was reaching down, his hand extended toward Miles.

"My apologies," said the monk.

It's a trick, Miles thought, and covered his face.

"I pray thee," said the monk, "stand up."

Miles slowly removed his hands from his face. The monk simply stood there, his hand extended. Miles did not move.

"Come now," said the monk. "I haven't all night."

Cautiously, Miles extended his right hand to the monk, who grabbed it and pulled him to his feet. The monk stood him upright and brushed him off.

"There—just as I found ye," said the monk, who

extended his right hand. "My name is Gallien."

Miles ached from top to bottom.

The welts on his back and side pounded with pain.

His breaths came in short, painful gasps.

All courtesy of the monk standing in front of him.

But, Miles realized, he had just been caught breaking into a church *and* destroying church property. As such, he considered it a far better approach to make peace with his attacker rather than argue over his own inconveniences. He took the monk's hand and shook it. "My name is Miles Letterford," he said, and paused. "Not to seem ungrateful, but may I ask why you relented?"

The monk gave a short laugh. "The ring, of course."

The ring.

The ring was why he was in this dark, dank stone church. The ring was why he had made this journey.

"You know of the ring?" asked Miles, suspiciously. "But how?" His friend had not mentioned that anyone else knew of the ring—or the box, for that matter.

"Aye," replied the monk. "Many years ago your friend—the man who once wore that ring—delivered that very box to me for safekeeping by the archangel."

The monk sensed Miles's uncertainty. "Fear not,

my friend. I swore an oath to watch over the box, but I have never asked its contents, nor sought to know them."

Miles breathed a sigh of relief. "Forgive my suspicions."

"No forgiveness is necessary," replied Gallien. "However, I fear that your journey brings bad tidings."

Miles nodded. "Indeed. He died a week ago."

The monk sighed. "When I saw the ring, I knew." His voice was heavy.

"Good monk," said Miles, "I must again seek your pardon for my actions this night. Had I known that you—"

"Nay," interrupted Gallien, "no pardon is necessary. I am pleased that the archangel has successfully fulfilled his duty."

The monk placed his hand on Miles's shoulder. His tone was solemn. "Now, my friend, that duty has fallen upon you. I pray thee, carry it well."

Miles looked back at the box. He knew what was inside and what it meant. For the first time, however, the weight—the significance—of this undertaking was clear to him.

Miles retrieved the box and carried it to the entrance of the church.

Gallien held open the door. "Do ye need assistance?" he asked.

"No," replied Miles. "It is a weight that I must bear."

The monk smiled in appreciation. "Then God keep ye, my friend."

Miles hoisted the box onto his shoulder and stepped out into the night.

England
Winter 1623

Ellis Hollensworth could not refuse the offer, as strange as it may have been.

It was more than he could earn in six months.

Six months? Gad! It was easily a year's pay.

Still, the ride had taken much longer than he had anticipated.

He had no idea where he was.

Had they left London and gone north? South? East? West?

He simply did not know.

For all he knew, he could still be in London. They may simply have been riding around in circles for hours.

The thick wool blindfold prevented him from seeing anything. It also covered his ears and muffled any sounds. Not that it mattered anyway. Heavy drapes covered the windows of the carriage. He had seen that much before the blindfold was put in place. The constant beat of the carriage wheels and the sound of the horse's hooves drowned out any other noise.

The carriage had stopped just minutes ago, and now he was being led somewhere. He could hear the dead winter grass crunch under his boots, and the faint sounds of flowing water in the distance. There was a slight but bone-chilling breeze.

Is it nighttime already? he thought. *How long have we been riding?*

"Stop," the voice said. And he did.

He could hear the heavy creaking of hinges.

A hand on his right forearm pulled him forward yet again.

Three steps forward, and his feet hit solid floor.

The wind stopped, but it was still cold. He was now inside some sort of structure. The hinges creaked again, and he heard the door shut.

THUD. Something heavy landed on the floor beside him. He assumed it was the device and his tools.

The instructions for the device had been very precise—they had made clear to him that there was no room for error. He had spent six months forging it.

Although he had constructed devices with similar components in the past, none of them approached the scale and complexity of the one that now sat—presumably—in a crate at his side. The customer had provided a single set of plans. When Ellis completed the work, the customer had demanded the return of the plans and an oath that they had not been copied.

He had placed the device and his tools in a wooden crate and, as instructed, waited to be picked up at the appointed hour. Now he was blindfolded and standing in some unknown structure in some unknown location in England.

The blindfold was removed. The light in the room—although represented by only a couple of lanterns—immediately blinded him. It took several minutes for his eyes to adjust before he could even squint at his surroundings. When he did, he discovered that he was in a small limestone room with a low ceiling. There were no markings in the room. No ornamentation. There was nothing to suggest where he was or the purpose of the room.

In front of him were the four horizontal limestone blocks into which the device would be fitted—just as the plans had indicated. Each block was exactly a foot and a half high and six feet wide. Although the blocks appeared massive, they were, in fact, barely five inches in thickness. And, critical to his particular task, each block was hollowed out, leaving a two-inch cavity that ran its length. When they were stacked one on top of another, the internal cavity would be exactly six feet high, five foot six inches in width, and exactly two inches in depth. The device was designed to fit into this cavity.

He began unpacking the crate. Slowly and precisely, he set each piece of the device into place in the cavity. The device had been made, in large part, of an alloy of bronze and gold. The metal was hard and expensive but would resist corrosion. The device was, he understood, intended to last for centuries.

Strange, though, he mused. *Built to last forever, but designed to be used only once.*

Finally, it was time for the central component.

The placement of the central component was critical. He slowly lowered it into place until the right and left sides clicked into position. From the box he retrieved an iron rod with a slightly concave tip. Placing the tip into a slot in the right side of the device, he gave a slight pull until he felt it click. He then moved back to the central component and inserted the tip of the iron rod into yet another slot.

This will not be as easy, he thought.

Taking a deep breath, he pulled hard on the iron rod. Slowly it began to move.

One click.

A second click.

A third click.

One more click, and the device would be set.

He pulled hard. The iron bar did not want to move. Despite the cold, he was sweating intensely.

And then, finally, when it appeared that it was not going to budge . . .

CLICK

It was done. Once the stones were put in place, the device would set itself until . . .

Until whenever.

SECRETS
OF
SHAKESPEARE'S
GRAVE

CHAPTER ONE
What News, I Prithee?

"CHANGE AT THE TOP FOR
PUBLISHING FIRM"
BY WALTER R. LICHAND
WALL STREET JOURNAL
JANUARY 24, 2005

For more than four hundred years, Letterford & Sons has published books of note

and distinction. Established in 1590 in London by Miles Letterford, the company had opened its first office in America in 1793 in New York City. Although Letterford & Sons is not the largest publisher in the world, many in the publishing community consider it the most prestigious. It remains a family-owned and -operated business. Yesterday, after forty years under the successful direction of Raymond Letterford, Jr., ownership of the company passed to his oldest son, Raymond "Mull" Letterford III. Mull Letterford has most recently served as vice president of business operations for the company. A ceremony celebrating the transition took place at the family's ancestral home in London.

"WAREHOUSE FIRE DESTROYS BOOK INVENTORY"

By ROJAS SMITH

LOS ANGELES TIMES

MAY 19, 2008

A fire broke out in a warehouse on Smaklin Street last night, destroying over ten thousand copies of the new book by author Debra Tavenhast. Tavenhast is the author of the wildly popular children's series about Tobby, the boy accountant. The books destroyed in the fire represented the entire first printing of her latest book, *Tobby Bridges the GAAP*. It was expected to be released on June 5. Mull Letterford, president of Letterford & Sons and the publisher of the series by Tavenhast, was not available for comment. The cause of the fire is unknown at this time and is under investigation.

"RECLUSIVE AUTHOR SIGNS CONTRACT
WITH DOUGHERTY HOUSE"
PUBLISHING TIMES
NEW YORK
JUNE 14, 2008

Dougherty House Publishing announced today that it has acquired the exclusive rights to publish the forthcoming novel by the reclusive and eccentric author Brogdon Honeycutt. Honeycutt, who has not appeared in public since the publication of his renowned novel *Concrete Monkey Hymns* in 1977, is reportedly receiving an advance of more than $3 million, half of which, he has insisted, must be paid in Mongolian Tugrik coins. The novel is expected to be ready for publication in time for the holiday shopping season. The signing of Honeycutt by Dougherty House ended one of the fiercest bidding wars between publishing houses in recent years. Mull Letterford, president of Letterford & Sons, expressed disappointment at his failure to acquire the rights to the new novel. The failure was a particularly hard blow to Letterford & Sons, which had published Honeycutt's famous 1977 novel. Honeycutt, who purportedly refuses to acknowledge the existence of Canada, released a two-word statement through his gardener regarding his agreement with Harvest House: "Pepper butterbottom."

Dougherty House offered no comment on the statement by its author.

"DEATH OF LOCAL PHILANTHROPIST STUNS COMMUNITY"

MANCHESTER STAR MERCURY

JULY 2, 2008

The sudden and unexpected death of Raymond Letterford, Jr., has shocked the Meriwether County community and the worldwide publishing community. Well known for his local philanthropic efforts, Raymond Letterford died of a heart attack at his family's home in Manchester on Monday, June 30. Letterford gained fame and fortune as the owner of Letterford & Sons, perhaps the most prestigious publishing company in the world.

CHAPTER TWO
Homeward Did They Bend Their Course

Manchester, Georgia
Wednesday, November 26
Late afternoon

Colophon Letterford took off her glasses, stuck her head out the open window of her father's car, and breathed deeply. The cool wind whipped across her face and through her shaggy blond hair.

Fall was far and away her favorite time of year. The mornings were cool enough to justify jeans and a light sweater; the afternoons were warm enough to accommodate shorts. The fall air smelled of dry grass and smoke from distant fireplaces, and the autumn sun painted the countryside with a warm ocher glaze. Colophon took it all in. It was perfect.

The moment, however, did not last.

"Hey, doofus, shut the frigging window. I'm freezing."

It was Case, Colophon's older brother and constant source of irritation. At fifteen, Case was three years older than Colophon. He had grown tall over the past year—at least two inches taller than their father—but this growth spurt had done little to mature him. He was the same bully that he had been a year before, only bigger and stronger.

Colophon kept her eyes closed and pretended that she hadn't heard her brother. This strategy didn't work. A quick punch to her left arm ensured that she paid attention.

"Jerk! You're not supposed to hit a girl."

"Bite me," he replied with a smirk.

Colophon shut the window, put her glasses back

on, and sat back in her seat as their father's car trundled lazily down the long driveway leading to their home in Manchester, Georgia. Colophon's great-great-grandfather had moved to Manchester in 1876. He had selected the small southern city because it shared the name of his mother's home-town in England, but not the cold and wet climate. Originally intended to serve as only a summer home, it eventually became the family's full-time residence.

The drive home from school had been unusual. As a general rule, their father was usually too busy to pick up Colophon and her brother from school. The family's publishing business occupied his time—now more than ever. Moreover, when her father did pick them up from school, he normally rambled on non-stop about some new manuscript that he was read-ing or a new book that would be coming out soon. Today, however, he remained silent as they drove home. Although his cell phone rang twice, he made no effort to answer it.

Colophon knew her father's company had recently suffered a series of mishaps, tragedies, and outright disasters—the loss of a best-selling author to a ri-val publishing house, a fire in a storage facility, and worst of all, the death of her grandfather. These events had led her father to be somewhat disengaged from family matters. Lately, he always seemed to be distracted. Case was, of course, oblivious to his father's mood. He passed the time on the drive home from school in his usual fashion—with earbuds in place and tethered to his iPod.

The driveway leading to the family home wound its way through a thick forest of tall hardwoods and then a large rolling field. Golden bales of freshly cut hay peppered the landscape. On both sides of the road, a low-stacked stone wall corralled the vehicle as it sped toward the large brick Victorian resting at the edge of the field. The three-story home was constructed of a dark red brick that had grown considerably darker over the last hundred years or so. A fine knit of fig ivy covered the tower at the front of the house.

As the vehicle turned into the pea gravel drive in front of the house, Colophon spied her mother waiting for them by the front door. Beside her sat Maggie, the family's golden retriever, her tail beating the ground in anxious anticipation.

Meg Letterford, Colophon's mother, was a small, thin woman with short, dusty-blond hair. A college professor by trade, she was as comfortable sitting on a tractor as she was teaching history behind a classroom podium. She had an earthy, outgoing quality that perfectly balanced her husband's bookish and scholarly demeanor.

Mull Letterford pulled to a stop. As Case and Colophon stepped out of the car, their mother greeted each of them with a hug and a kiss on the cheek. Case, in usual teenage fashion, shrugged off his mother's affections, although his efforts appeared halfhearted at best.

"Any homework?" asked Meg Letterford.

"No," replied Colophon. "We have all of Thanksgiving off—no homework and no assigned reading!"

"Pity. I'm sure I could come up with something, if you like? Perhaps a call to one of your teachers for some suggestions?"

Colophon feigned shock. "Mom!"

"Very well," Meg Letterford replied in mock exasperation. "Rot your brains with TV and video games—see if I care."

"You know better," Colophon said.

"Indeed I do," replied Meg, who was intensely proud of her daughter's academic efforts.

Meg bent over and whispered in Colophon's ear: "How was your father on the way home from school?"

Colophon could hear the concern in her mother's voice. "Quiet," she replied.

Meg sighed deeply.

"Is everything OK?" asked Colophon.

Her mother stood up straight. "Just business, that's all. It's been tough lately. It has him distracted."

Colophon looked into her mother's eyes. She could sense there was more going on than she was willing to say. She started to ask, but her mother interrupted.

"This, too, shall pass," she said. "Let's have a happy Thanksgiving break, OK?"

Chapter Three

My Books ... Shall Be My Company

Colophon walked down the long entrance hallway, past the library, to the stairs that led to her room on the second floor. At the end of the entrance hallway, on the wall opposite the stairs, Miles Letterford stared down at her from a large, ornately framed portrait. The painting had always given Colophon the creeps. In the portrait, Miles Letterford sat in front of a window, a book in his hands, and stared angrily at the viewer. Despite her father's assurances that Miles had been considered a rather nice fellow, Colophon remained firmly unconvinced.

Colophon's room, located down a short passage at the top of the second-floor stairs, overlooked the front of the house. It was large, painted bright blue, with an exceedingly high ceiling. After tossing her book bag onto her bed, she grabbed her laptop and headed back downstairs to the family's library.

The library was, far and away, Colophon's favorite room in the house. Entering it was like stepping into an old sepia-toned photograph—it was timeless. The room gave no overt hint that it existed in the twenty-first century.

Two stories tall and equally wide, the library's considerable size belied its coziness. From the center of the ceiling hung an enormous half-dome light that cast a soft amber glow throughout the room. The wide oak flooring, which had aged warmly over the years into a deep, rich reddish brown, creaked slightly as Colophon took a step. She closed her eyes and took a deep breath. The room smelled of dust, old paper, and pipe tobacco. It was, in her estimation, quite wonderful.

She walked over to one of the massive oak bookcases and ran her fingers across the leather spines of several books. She had grown up around this vast collection, and the titles (at least those at her eye level) were as familiar to her as her family's names. A copy of every book ever published by Letterford & Sons was kept in the room. In fact, shortly after construction of the house, the entire Letterford library from London—including all of Miles Letterford's personal volumes—had been shipped to Manchester to be included in the collection. The room itself was a precise copy of the family library in London.

A large stone fireplace occupied a sizable portion of the library's far wall. Above the fireplace and mounted on the wall was a tellurion, a large mechanical device designed to show the motions of the earth and the moon around the sun.

Anchoring one side of the library were two enormous oak tables with brass reading lamps and heavy wooden chairs. A massive oriental rug, tea-stained through age and use, covered the middle of the room. At the edges of the rug sat four large, well-worn leather chairs. Squatting in the center of the rug was an enormous coffee table stacked impossibly high with books, manuscripts, and various items of indeterminate nature.

Four massive bookcases flanked the fireplace. The first bookcase, to the far left of the fireplace, was occupied only by vellum-covered books from the fifteenth and sixteenth centuries. Their spines looked like the skins of mummies, drawn dry and tight with age, revealing the bones beneath. As the books were both creepy and written primarily in Latin and other languages that she did not read, Colophon had spent little time exploring them. The books and bookcases progressed through the centuries from left to right and from top to bottom. Familiar titles and authors—first editions all—filled every shelf.

Colophon's favorite part of the room was the "curiosity shelf" that was built into the wall on the left side of the room. The items on this particular shelf had been collected by members of her family for hundreds of years. They were fossils of every size and shape, dinosaur teeth, ancient timepieces, strange glass orbs, an old type set, political buttons, small framed autographs of famous and not-so-famous authors, at least two swords, a carved wooden fish from Pitcairn Island, an odd little machine made of brass devised for the apparent purpose of crimping paper, old sporting trophies, ancient coins, Bronze Age spear points, and numerous other oddities and artifacts. As if to complement this odd collection, in the corner of the room sat a large copper pot that contained an assortment of ancient wooden golf clubs, several cricket bats, a field hockey stick, an old wooden lacrosse stick, two warped wooden tennis rackets, and a pair of wooden skis. The books, antiquities, and artifacts that filled the library were a constant marvel and delight to Colophon.

She closed the library doors, took her seat at one of the oak tables, and opened up her laptop.

Technically speaking, she had told her mother the truth—she did not have any homework to complete over the Thanksgiving holiday. However, she did have an extra-credit assignment. Her history teacher, Mrs. Eager, had offered ten bonus points for every student who wrote a short essay on Eleanor Roosevelt over the Thanksgiving break. Piece of cake—history was Colophon's favorite subject. And an essay on Eleanor Roosevelt? Icing on the cake. Colophon loved reading about Eleanor Roosevelt and her husband, President Franklin D. Roosevelt. After all, President and Mrs. Roosevelt had spent more than their fair share of time at a small cottage in Warm Springs—not more than a mile from where Colophon now lived—known as the Little White House. Colophon could write this essay in her sleep.

Colophon had not said anything to her mother about the extra-credit assignment because she knew that her brother would tease her mercilessly, particularly since she was doing bonus work.

She got enough teasing already from Case. She certainly didn't need any more, thank you.

After about half an hour of peace and quiet, Colophon heard the door to the library creak open. She looked up and saw her brother entering the room.

Can't he just leave me alone? she thought. She shut her laptop.

"Hey, dipstick, whatcha doing?"

"None of your business, Case."

He walked over to the table and flipped the laptop back open.

"Leave my computer alone!" she snapped.

Ignoring his sister's protests, he bent over and looked at the screen.

"A report? You are actually working on a report for school? You are on vacation. V-A-C-A-T-I-O-N. Vacation. You are such a dork."

Colophon slammed the laptop back shut. "You are such a . . . jerk!"

"Ow. That hurt. Really, I'm hurting. I suppose you're also looking forward to tomorrow's dorkfest for Thanksgiving, aren't you?"

"As a matter of fact, I am," replied Colophon. "I'm sorry our family is not more exciting. Perhaps our parents might be willing to find you a new home at a distant military school?"

"Again, that hurt. I probably won't sleep tonight because of that cruel comment. You wound me."

Colophon grabbed her laptop and stomped out of the library. She headed directly for the kitchen. A cookie (or two) wouldn't make her brother vanish, but it wouldn't hurt either. As she turned down the hallway leading to the kitchen, she passed her father's office. The door was slightly ajar, and she could here voices from within. She paused. One voice was her father's, and he did not sound happy. In fact, he seemed very angry.

"You cannot be serious!" her father thundered.

"But I am," said a deep, calm voice. "Very serious."

The voices mingled, and Colophon heard heavy footsteps heading toward the door. She quickly moved down the hallway and around the corner, then stopped with her back against the wall and listened.

"We will talk again tomorrow," said the deep voice. "I suggest that you accept the situation."

Colophon braved a peek around the corner and saw a tall, thin bald man in a dark suit striding toward the front door of the house. The door to her father's office shut quickly.

CHAPTER FOUR
The Ill Wind Which Blows

The female voice rang from the kitchen into the hall-way: "If I catch you in this kitchen one more time, young lady, you will become close and personal friends with my spatula. You will eat when the whole family eats and not a minute sooner. Do I make myself clear?"

Audrey Letterford handed her niece Colophon a plate of cookies and said in a hushed tone, "Do you think your mother heard me?"

"I think everyone in the house heard you," replied Colophon with a grin.

Audrey Letterford chuckled. "Well, they are used to that. Anyway, it's a holiday, for goodness' sake, and I've been in this kitchen cooking all day. If your favorite aunt wants to give you some cookies, what is my little brother going to do about it? Nothing, that's what. Now get out of here, and don't let anyone see you."

"Thanks, Aunt Audrey. You're the best," said Colophon as she scooted out the back door.

Colophon made her way through the garden and headed toward the lake. At the edge of the lake and shielded from the house by a large, slightly overgrown hedgerow was a small metal bench. She sat down on the bench, unwrapped the plate, and started in on the large pumpkin spice cookie on top.

As she sat eating her cookie, a shadow passed over her head and out over the lake. She looked up and spied a large silver hawk circling lazily in the sky. Hawks were common around the family's home and could frequently be spied circling the hay fields as they hunted for mice, snakes, and rabbits. It occurred to her, however, that she had never seen a hawk above the lake. She nibbled on her cookie and watched as the large bird drifted on the breeze that constantly blew down from the mountain and across the water. The hawk's wings rarely moved as it dipped and turned with the air currents. Its reflection shimmered in the water as it passed over the far side of the lake.

It was mesmerizing.

Dreamlike.

As Colophon watched, the hawk turned in a long slow arc and headed back across the lake in her direction. Just as it reached her side of the lake, the large bird tucked its wings and went into a steep dive. Colophon froze.

The hawk was heading straight for her.

The bird came closer and closer. At the last second, it adjusted its dive ever so slightly and splashed into the lake just a few feet from where she sat. There was a small explosion of water, then the hawk took flight back across the lake, tucked low against the surface. As it flew away, Colophon could see a large snake writhing to get free of the hawk's claws.

Colophon's heart beat rapidly as the hawk disappeared into the stand of hardwoods on the far side of the lake. For the moment, the cookies were completely forgotten, as was her brother.

The moment, however, did not last long. Footsteps crunched to her left on the pea gravel path.

Case! Why couldn't he leave her alone?

She grabbed the cookies and scooted into an opening in the hedgerow. She sat still and listened. The footsteps stopped. A moment later the smell of cigarette smoke drifted into and through the thick foliage. To her knowledge, no member of her immediate family smoked. She did not move.

A deep voice—the same deep voice that she had heard in her father's office—broke the silence.

"He responded as I expected he would."

Silence again.

Colophon sat frozen.

"No. I did not think that he would simply turn the company over to me."

Another pause.

The deep voice: "You've done well—as I expected. It's only a matter of time now. Needless to say, the resources are not and will not be available to him to solve this problem. Now I have to get back to the house. We will speak again tomorrow evening. I expect everything to be resolved by that time."

Colophon could hear a faint beep signaling the end of the call.

And then there was silence again.

She knew the deep-voiced man remained on the other side of the hedge. Finally, she saw a cigarette butt hit the edge of the lake and fizzle slightly. And then silence, except for the wind rustling through the woods near the lake.

She sat absolutely still and listened intently. After a minute or so, having heard nothing, she stuck her head out from the small opening to look around. She did not see anything and ventured farther out.

Looking back up the path to the house, she saw no one.

Colophon turned to pick up her cookies—and there standing directly in front of her was the man from her father's office. He was tall, bald, and thin, as she remembered. His piercing black eyes peered down at her over dark, thick-rimmed glasses. And, she noticed, he had no eyebrows, which she found very unsettling.

"I assume," he said in his deep voice, "that your parents taught you that it is impolite to listen to other people's conversations?"

"I didn't . . . I just came down here to have some cookies."

The man looked down at the cookies in Colophon's hand. "Of course you did," he said. "What was I thinking? My apologies."

The tall man's tone was less than warm.

He bent down and looked Colophon directly in the eyes. She couldn't move. She could smell the cigarettes on his breath. His black eyes bored into her. He slowly raised his hand. She watched as the man's long index finger approached her face.

His placed his finger on the side of her face and then lightly flicked the side of her mouth.

"You missed a crumb," he said.

Colophon turned and ran as fast as she could back to the house.

Chapter Five
Under Thy Own Life's Key

Colophon pushed open the door to her father's office and stuck her head inside. Mull Letterford was on the phone but motioned for her to enter. Her heart was still racing from the encounter by the lake, but she focused on trying to calm herself. She looked around the small room. The walls were covered with a dizzying array of black-and-white photos of her family. None of the frames seemed to match, and there was no particular pattern in the arrangement. Immediately behind her father's desk was a small photo of her grandfather holding a young Mull Letterford on his knee. Colophon missed her grandfather. This had once been his office, and she could still smell the smoke from his pipe. She was glad her

father had left the office in essentially the same con-
dition as her grandfather had kept it.

On her father's desk and under a small glass cover
was a brass key that had once belonged to Miles
Letterford. It had been passed down from her grandfather to her father as a symbol of the ownership of
the company.

Colophon scooted her chair quietly up to the desk
and leaned in to look at the key. It was a passkey,
no more than three inches long, with the name
Letterford inscribed down the shank. The tooth of the
key was a simple square. The bow of the key—the
end that is turned—was oval-shaped with the Greek
letter sigma—Σ—engraved in the middle. Colophon
moved closer to the key, her breath lightly fogging
the glass.

It was hard to believe that the key would one day
be passed down to her obnoxious brother.

The phone clicked down into the receiver, and she
looked up. "Are you busy?" she asked her father.

"Never too busy for you. So what brings you to the
office?"

Mull Letterford appeared tired. He was sitting
in a large rocking chair. On his desk were stacks of
manuscripts for his review. She could tell, however,

that he had not been reading them, and that his mind was on something else altogether.

"Dad, may I ask you a question?"

"Certainly. You know you can ask me anything."

"You do own Letterford and Sons, don't you? I mean, it's your business, isn't it?"

His response was measured. "It is my business, but it is also the family's business."

"What do you mean?" asked Colophon.

"I own the majority interest in the business. That means I have total control over the operations of the publishing house. However, and this is very important, I also have an obligation to the family. It is an obligation passed down from generation to generation. When your grandfather turned ownership of the business over to me, I assumed a responsibility that has been required of every owner of Letterford and Sons."

"What responsibility?"

"We operate the business for the family. I may own the majority interest in Letterford and Sons— just as your grandfather did and his father before him and so on and so on—but we have employed generations of the family in a variety of jobs. Miles Letterford had four sons. He could have left the business to all of them. But that would've been a mess.

He understood—as too few do, I might add—that passing ownership to all of his children would ultimately have proven a disaster and resulted in the destruction of the company and the family. He had to choose some way of deciding who would run the company. Ownership had to pass according to some rule. He elected to pass the business to his eldest son and to obligate all future owners to do the same. Miles's three other sons were each granted a small ownership interest in the company, which they in turn have passed down over the generations. Control of the company, however, was vested in Miles's oldest son. This was a harsh and an arbitrary decision. I am not suggesting otherwise. Rules such as this are always arbitrary. However, they are also necessary."

Mull paused, took a sip of coffee, and stared out the window at the field outside.

"I have no misconceptions as to how I became owner of the family business. It wasn't by merit. I didn't earn it. It was simply by virtue of when I was born. That, I believe, places an even greater obligation on me. I am responsible to the other members of the family for the operations of the business. Their livelihoods depend on me doing my job and doing it well. It can be a heavy burden at times."

Colophon walked over and stood beside her father.

"Could the business ever be taken from you?"

He looked at his daughter. "Why do you ask?"

"I heard that man talking to you—the tall man in your office earlier today. I wasn't eavesdropping, I promise. Are you mad at me?"

He smiled. "No. I suspect half the household heard that conversation."

"Who was he?"

He paused and took another sip of his coffee. "That was someone I have known for a long time."

"A friend?"

"No." Her father's voice was firm.

"Then who—" she started.

Mull Letterford placed his hand on his daughter's shoulder. "That, my dear, is all you need to know for right now. Besides, it's almost time for dinner, and I am absolutely sure"—he added with a slight wink—"that you haven't done anything to spoil your dinner. Correct?" And with that, Colophon understood their conversation had ended.

CHAPTER SIX
Be Bounteous at Our Meal

Thanksgiving Dinner
Thursday, November 27

For the first time in her life, Colophon was allowed to sit at the adult table for Thanksgiving dinner. Unfortunately, her brother was not making this an easy transition.

Tradition in the Letterford family dictated that children younger than twelve years ate together at a table in a room adjacent to the dining room. Since

Colophon had now reached the age of twelve, she was permitted to join the adult table. Seating here was not random; rather, it was assigned according to a strict family hierarchy. Mull, as the owner of Letterford & Sons, sat at the head of the table. Mrs. Letterford sat to his right. Immediately to their right and left sat Mull's two brothers and their spouses, and then aunts, uncles, cousins, and so on. At the far end of the table and almost immediately opposite her father sat Colophon. Next to her sat her cousin Jules, who had turned twelve the preceding year and was therefore enjoying his second year at the adult table. Next to Jules sat his older brother Patrick, and next to Patrick was Colophon's brother, Case.

Colophon remembered the years she had watched and envied her brother as he sat at the table with the adults. Although Case took no particular pleasure in being in the presence of the adults, he relished the idea that his mere presence at the adult table drove his sister absolutely crazy. He would often find an excuse to stop by the children's room during the course of dinner just to remind Colophon that he was at the adult table and she sat among the toddlers. Colophon had hoped things would improve once she reached the adult table. She was wrong. Her brother was merciless in his quips and comments about her. Jules and Patrick snickered at each of Case's insults. Colophon tried to ignore the insults and her cousins' reactions, but it was not easy.

Dinner, per family tradition, began with a prayer from the youngest member at the main table. As such, the duty today fell upon Colophon. The previous year Jules had made it halfway through his prayer before vomiting on the table from nervousness. The cleanup had delayed dinner by half an hour. That was the only year that Colophon had been happy to be seated in the children's dining room. Now, although nervous, she took her duty seriously. In a precise and dignified manner, she managed to say grace over the food they were about to receive—without vomiting. A round of congratulations on a job well done quickly followed. He father looked at her and silently mouthed the word "outstanding." Her mother gave a thumbs-up.

The moment, however, did not last long. "At least Jules didn't put me to sleep when he threw up last year," Case whispered in Colophon's direction. "I thought the nap was supposed to come after dinner, not during the prayer."

Jules and Patrick busted out laughing. A disapproving glance from the far end of the table brought an end to the laughter, but the damage was done. Colophon stared straight ahead, furious at her brother and her cousins.

It took several minutes for the food to be served, and just as those gathered had started to eat, a tall, thin, unshaven man with glasses and long stringy hair burst into the room. He was dressed in a threadbare sweater, which at one time might have been some shade of light yellow. His pants were bright blue corduroy and equally worn, with patches on both knees. On top of his head was a black wool beanie, and under his arms he carried an assortment of rolled-up documents. He looked as if he hadn't slept (or bathed) for days.

After surveying the family gathered at the table, the oddly dressed man exclaimed in a loud voice, "Mull, I must see you immediately!"

Without looking up from his food, Mull Letterford replied: "Cousin Julian, it is so nice that you have finally arrived. You realize, I assume, that it is Thanksgiving and that we are gathered here for Thanksgiving dinner?"

The odd man looked around the room. "Is it Thanksgiving already?" said Julian with apparent confusion.

"Yes, Julian, it is Thanksgiving already," Mull said

calmly as he gestured to the family and then to the turkey that sat in the middle of the table.

"Well, I . . . but . . . I must—" protested the new arrival.

Mull Letterford held up his hand. "What you must do is wait until we finish dinner before we discuss anything. Please, have a seat and join us. I insist. There is an open chair at the end of the table." Mull gestured to the empty seat next to Colophon.

For several moments Julian considered his options with a look of uncertainty. He ran his hand across the thick stubble on his face as if he were contemplating some great and significant point. The entire family stared at him, with knives, forks, and spoons frozen in place.

The room was quiet, as if someone had pushed a pause button on some grand remote control. Finally, realizing that everyone was looking at him, and apparently facing the reality that nothing would be done until after dinner, the unkempt man dropped everything that he had been holding and sat down in the empty seat next to Colophon. The sounds of the meal immediately started up again.

Under his breath, Julian muttered: "Thanksgiving dinner? I can't believe I barged in on Thanksgiving dinner. Smooth. Real smooth. Nice going, Julian."

"Hello," Colophon interrupted.

The unshaven man turned and peered down at her over the top of his glasses, then turned his gaze to the empty plate in front of him.

Colophon prickled at the man's rude reaction. It was bad enough that she had to put up with her brother's insults and her cousins' laughter, but who was this so-called cousin? He looked like he hadn't shaved in days! And to burst in on Thanksgiving dinner—that took some nerve.

Colophon, however, took a deep breath. She knew her mother and father expected more from her. Perhaps the gentleman had simply not heard her. She would try again. "Hello," she repeated, in a friendly voice.

Again, the disheveled man turned to Colophon and peered down at her. "Hello," he grunted.

She stuck out her right hand. "My name is Colophon Letterford."

"I thought this was the adult table," Julian replied. He ignored her outstretched hand.

"Excuse me?"

"Excuse what?"

"What did you mean that you thought this was the adult table?" Colophon asked.

"I said I thought this was the adult table. At least that used to be the rule."

"I am twelve years old," Colophon responded. "I am allowed at this table."

With an impatient shake of his head, Julian bent over to Colophon, stared directly into her eyes, and said: "No disrespect, and I sincerely mean that, but I am really not in the mood for this conversation." He then turned back to his plate.

Colophon stared straight ahead.

How rude!

For years she had sat at the children's table and waited patiently for her chance to sit at the adult table. It was her time to sit at the adult table, and no one was going to treat her like a toddler—least of all this obnoxious man.

Colophon therefore persisted with the conversation. "My father is Mull Letterford. Does he know why you want to speak with him?"

"Yes," Julian replied, "I suspect he does."

"Then maybe I will simply ask him why you are here. It certainly sounded very exciting when you burst into the room."

Colophon started to raise her hand to wave at her father.

"No—wait."

She dropped her hand.

Julian leaned back in his chair. "If you must know . . ."

"I must," insisted Colophon.

"I need to examine the portrait of Miles Letterford that hangs in the foyer." He turned back to his plate.

"Why do you need to see it?"

"Do you suffer from some sort of obsessive-compulsive disorder?"

Colophon ignored the insult. "Why do you need to see the painting? It's rather dreary."

Julian turned impatiently to Colophon, bent over, and whispered, "It is not a concern for children. Now, please eat your vegetables and be a good little girl."

Colophon stared at the newcomer. "I always eat my vegetables."

Keeping her eyes directly on this so-called Cousin Julian, she started to raise her hand again to get her father's attention.

"No, please don't," whispered Julian.

Colophon lowered her hand again. Julian closed his eyes and ran his hands through his stringy hair.

"You have to understand," he whispered to her, "this is not a topic for conversation around this table.

You may have noticed that I don't exactly fit in with the crowd around here. Please, I've been subject to enough ridicule by the family already."

As have I, thought Colophon. But she recognized that the urgency and concern in his voice was real. Her frustration over being treated like a small child quickly passed.

"Why would anyone make fun of you?" she asked.

"Honestly, look at me. I'm unkempt and unshaven. My hair is long. I don't wear suits, ties, or cardigans. *And* perhaps most important, I don't work in the family business. That makes me a bit of a crackpot, I suppose," he replied.

"My brother makes fun of me, and I don't care for it one bit. I think it is quite rude."

Julian leaned back in his chair and put his fork down. He pulled his glasses off and cleaned them with his napkin. He replaced his glasses and turned back to Colophon.

"You will have to accept my apologies for my initial rudeness. My skin is not as thick as it once was. The years have left me a bit testy. Let's try this again, shall we?"

Julian sat up straight, and extended his right hand to Colophon. "Please allow me to introduce myself. I am Julian Letterford, your father's first cousin. It is a pleasure to meet you."

Colophon took Julian's right hand and shook it. "And my name is Colophon Letterford. It is likewise a pleasure to make your acquaintance."

Chapter Seven
To Me Thy Secrets Tell

Julian excused himself from the dinner table shortly after the plates were removed. Colophon had seen him engaged in a brief conversation with her father and then lost track of him. Shortly after dessert was served—a wonderful bread pudding—Colophon made her way to the front of the house to the portrait of Miles Letterford. There she found Julian standing in front of the painting. His face was pressed close to it behind a large magnifying glass. Colophon stood directly behind him straining to see what he was examining.

"And what do you make of it?" Julian's voice startled her.

Julian repeated, "Well, what do you make of it?" He remained bent over with his face pressed against the magnifying glass.

"To be honest, I've never really looked at it all that close. It's creepy. I wish my father would remove it."

"He can't remove it."

"What do you mean?" Colophon asked. Of course he could remove it. This was his house.

Julian stood back from the painting and looked down at her. "Are you telling me that you don't know about the portrait?"

She shook her head. "No. Am I supposed to know about it?"

"Yes. Absolutely. It is a critical part of your family's history."

Julian paused briefly, looked down the hallway, and then leaned over to Colophon.

"Very well," he whispered, "I guess it's up to me. The portrait was painted by Dimplert Steumacher, an obscure portrait painter in the early seventeenth century in England. Have you heard of him?"

Colophon shook her head.

"The fact that you haven't heard of him is certainly not a knock against you. Poor Dimplert's fame has not extended into the twenty-first century."

He stood back and gestured toward the painting.

"Dimplert painted portraits. He painted this particular portrait on commission by Miles Letterford. It's a very nice example of his work as a portraitist. However, it is much more than that. In his last will and testament, Miles Letterford decreed that the portrait must always hang in the home of the company's current owner."

"Always?"

"And forever. It is, if you will, one of the marks of ownership."

"Like the key," Colophon said.

"Yes, exactly," replied Julian. "This portrait has been passed down from Letterford to Letterford for generations."

Colophon stared up at it. "Miles Letterford must have had quite the ego if he wanted his portrait to be hung forever."

"Perhaps," Julian replied. "Most members of the family certainly seem to think so. That's why they think he required it to be hung in this manner—so everyone would be reminded of who started the company."

He turned and looked at her. "I can assure you, however, that they are wrong. There is another explanation."

"Which is . . . ?"

"Look at the frame."

Colophon moved close to the painting and looked up at the frame. It was quite thick. The wood had darkened over the centuries into a deep brown—almost black—color. It smelled like dust. In the top corners of the frame were round wooden medallions. A third medallion was located at the bottom of and at the center of the frame. Carved into the medallions were the profiles of three men. The rest of the frame appeared to be some sort of intricately carved scrollwork.

"Looks the same as it always has. Creepy."

Julian lightly ran his finger along the carved scrollwork. "You're not seeing what's directly in front of you."

Colophon moved closer to the frame. As had Julian,

she ran her index finger along the scrollwork. "Just a bunch of squiggles and lines." She looked at her finger and corrected herself: "Dusty squiggles and lines."

"Ah, but wait." Julian walked a short way down the hall and flicked off the switch for the hallway light. The hallway turned dark.

"Well, that helps," said Colophon. "Now I can't see it at all."

Julian cut on a small flashlight. "Here, let's see if this helps." He pointed the light at the top of the frame.

Colophon noticed that the woodwork on the frame was not uniform in depth. Parts of it were deeper recessed than others. As Julian moved the flashlight across the frame, a pattern appeared—a pattern that Colophon instantly recognized. Recessed within the elaborate scrollwork—and almost hidden within the pattern—were letters. Although she had been around the painting her entire life, she had never noticed the letters, carved delicately into the detail of the frame.

"Letters," Colophon said.

Julian pulled over a chair. "Stand on the chair. Hold the flashlight and start reading from the top."

Starting from the top of the frame and moving the flashlight clockwise, Colophon read:

> *"Good friend among the stars be found,*
> *A treasure—heare the key thus bound.*
> *Blesed be the man who lays the claime,*
> *To that encloased within this frame."*

Colophon stepped off the chair, as Julian turned the lights back on.

"It seems to have an awful lot of misspellings."

"Perhaps for our day and age, but four hundred years ago it would have been perfectly acceptable. Now, aside from the spelling, what catches your attention?"

Colophon turned back to the frame. The words had disappeared back into the scrollwork as if by magic.

"It mentioned a treasure . . . ?"

"Precisely."

"What treasure?"

"The family treasure, of course."

Colophon looked up at him. "Whoa, hold on. I didn't know we had a family treasure. That's awesome."

"Yes, yes, I quite agree. Awesome indeed."

"So how come I haven't heard about this treasure?"

Julian sighed. He seemed to sigh a lot. "Most of

the family believes that Miles Letterford was actually referring to himself as the 'treasure' of the family—an ego boast of sorts."

Colophon looked back at the picture. Suddenly it didn't seem quite so creepy.

"And what do you think?"

"I think otherwise," replied Julian. "The problem —as I see it—is that Miles did not have a reputation of having a grand ego. Quite the opposite in fact. He was a humble, hard-working, and highly intelligent man. It doesn't make sense. Why hang it in the house? How many people will actually see it in a house? Why not a college or library? He was a distinguished graduate of Trinity College. Why not there? Donate some money in your will, and BAM, the portrait is hung in some hallway in perpetuity. No. He didn't do that. He wanted it hung in his home."

"Maybe he wanted to keep an eye on his family," Colophon said with a sly smile.

Julian ignored her comment. "Based on reading his papers, Miles appears to have been quite jovial, good-natured, and generous. His papers document numerous loans that he made to keep businesses afloat, to pay off debts, and for other reasons. It's hard to tell if any of those loans were ever repaid. Considering the favorable terms of the loans, I suspect most, if not all, were forgiven. He gave to numerous charities. He was a supporter of the arts."

Julian paused and stared at the painting.

"No, Miles Letterford was not some raving egomaniac. The inscription doesn't make sense based on what we actually know about him. I believe the inscription—placed there by Miles—refers to something else. A real treasure."

"What type of treasure?"

Julian paused again. "That's just it," he finally replied, his tone apologetic. "I'm not sure. I have my theories, but that's all they are—theories. Many members of this family have ruined themselves by obsessing over the poem in a quest for treasure. I suspect your father thinks I am heading down that same path. That's probably why you have heard nothing of the treasure—or of me."

Colophon nodded in agreement. "I don't think my father would approve."

Julian turned back to face the painting. "Pity. It would have been interesting to see his bright mind attack this mystery."

Colophon likewise turned back to the painting and stared at it. "So, you really believe it's a treasure map?"

"Yes."

"And where has that treasure map led you?" asked Colophon.

"Everywhere and nowhere." Julian turned and faced her. "You'll have to excuse my self-pity. I tend to indulge myself at times, often at the expense of those around me. So tell me, what do you see in the painting? Anything jump out at you?"

Colophon looked up at her great-great-great-great grandfather's visage. The painting had darkened significantly with age and now had a soft amber glaze. A vast web of thin cracks covered the surface.

In the painting, Miles Letterford, who appeared to be around seventy years old, sat in front of a large window that framed a night sky full of stars. He was posed behind a table. In his hands, he held a large book. Colophon could not make out the cover due to the darkening of the painting. On the table were scattered several type sets—small engraved blocks of wood used for printing at the time Miles was alive. On the wall to his right and at the very edge of the painting was what appeared to be a round silver object. Numerous other items were sprinkled throughout the painting.

"Well?" asked Julian.

"If it's a treasure map, there seem to be a lot of potential clues."

"For example?"

"Well, there are the wooden blocks."

"The type set."

"Yes," replied Colophon. "The type set. They seem like a fairly obvious clue. I doubt that they were included simply for interest. I suspect they mean something."

"Anything else?"

"Well, there is the book. I can't quite make out its title." She paused. "To be honest with you," she finally said, "the painting seems filled with objects that could all be clues."

"Yes, all of those items could be clues—or not. The problem with this painting is not identifying the clues. The problem is trying to figure out what they mean—if anything."

"Well, does the type set spell anything?"

Julian threw his hands into the air. "Oh, they spell out all sorts of stuff. Trust me, I have spent any number of evenings rearranging those letters. But I am afraid that my efforts have led nowhere."

"Then is it a code of some sort?"

"Perhaps, but what type of code? Some form of cipher? Is it the key to the code or the code itself? I have tried to match the letters against numerous codes. Nothing fits. I'm sure there is a code hidden somewhere in this picture. I just can't figure it out."

This particular confession seemed to deflate him. "To be honest with you, most—well, perhaps all—of the family believes that I am a bit odd for pursuing the treasure."

"My brother thinks I am odd."

"Well," replied Julian, "I'm hardly one to judge, am I?"

"My brother wants to sit around all day and listen to his iPod, play video games, and slowly turn into a vegetable. I like to read. I like to write. I like to draw. And I enjoy school. If that makes me odd, so be it."

"Well put," replied Julian.

Colophon and Julian stared at the painting in silence for several moments.

Colophon interrupted the silence. "So, you never explained why you came here this evening to look at the painting."

"Well, as you can see, there are a lot of details that are difficult to discern. After the painting was completed, a glaze was brushed all across the surface to give it a uniform finish. Unfortunately, over time, that glaze has yellowed, darkened, and cracked. This painting has hung over fireplaces and has been exposed to smoke and soot for a couple of centuries and more. That's why it's so dark. Most people don't realize how brilliant the colors originally were in these old paintings. Did you know, for example, that many people, including art historians, opposed the cleaning of the Sistine Chapel because they were so used to the haze, smoke, and soot that covered it? When it was cleaned, it was brilliant, as Michelangelo intended. Details that had been lost for centuries were revealed. The same is true here. I hoped that the painting hid secrets. I thought that there may be clues in the shadows that would help me in deciphering the painting and that by examining the painting a little closer I could see if any hidden details emerged. The shadows, however, appear to hide nothing."

"So what will you do next?"

"I will do as I have always done. I will ponder and obsess over the clues and what they mean. I will rearrange the type set for the one millionth time. I will continue to read about Miles Letterford. I will look at the problem from all sides. That's all I can do."

He looked down at Colophon.

"Now, my dear, I must make my way out of your house. I am afraid that I have imposed on your family far too much this evening. Please express my thanks to your father and mother for dinner and for allowing me to examine the painting. And thank you for your company. It has truly been a pleasure."

And with that, Julian placed his cap on his head, gathered his collection of documents under his arm, and headed down the hallway to the entrance.

Colophon turned back to the painting and stared at it again.

CHAPTER EIGHT
To Desperate Ventures

Colophon sat in a small chair at the top of the stairs on the library's second floor. She was paging through a large book of portrait painters from the sixteenth century when she heard the large oak doors to the library open. Peering over the rail, she saw her father enter the room. She could tell that he was angry and started to ask him what was wrong when the tall man from the lake suddenly followed him into the room. The tall man was, in turn, followed by several other members of her family and finally by her great-uncle Portis Letterford. Colophon silently slipped from her chair and crouched behind the large vase that stood in the corner. She could hear the doors shut, although she could not see what was happening.

"I cannot believe you are even suggesting this!" Mull Letterford said in a loud and angry voice.

"You give us no choice," the deep voice from the lake responded calmly. "Your sales are down. The business is suffering."

"The business is not suffering," her father responded. "No one could have foreseen what has happened over the last year. Certainly, it has had an effect on the company. But the company will recover. It's money that you're concerned about. The business of Letterford is sound. Why, even with the tragedies of this year, we published two award-winning books, one that was a finalist for the Pulitzer."

"And how many copies of these award-winning books were sold?" asked the deep voice.

"Not many," replied one of the cousins, "not many at all."

Colophon could hear a general murmur of agreement.

"And but for a series of disasters—all outside my control—we would not be in this room having this discussion," said Mull.

There was a pause. Then the deep voice replied, "True. But the books did burn. And"—the deep voice paused for effect—"you, not I or anyone else in this room, failed to re-sign one of the most important authors of the past half-century. It is a business. The Letterford name has value."

"It also has respect and tradition," interrupted Mull Letterford. "That, Treemont, is something you simply do not understand."

Treemont! Colophon thought. *The tall man from the lake is named Treemont.*

"Respect does not sell books," Treemont responded. "Tradition does not pay the bills. The family cannot reasonably be expected to allow you to remain in your position without some realistic expectation that the business will turn around immediately."

No one spoke for a long moment.

"I have the votes of the family to invoke the clause," Treemont finally said.

There was silence.

"The clause," Uncle Portis finally said, "can only be

invoked at the meeting of the family that occurs on Christmas Eve—no sooner."

"You are correct," answered Treemont. "That means that Mull has just under a month before the clause is invoked."

"One month?" said Mull. "But...that's impractical."

The deep voice responded: "One month is all the family can offer. I suggest you use the time to get your affairs in order."

Colophon heard the shuffling of chairs below. She peeked around the vase and saw the tall man rise from his chair and straighten his coat. He then turned to Mull Letterford.

"Of course, you always have the right to purchase the interests of the three other families."

Mull offered a mock laugh. "You know as well as I do that the price is far too high. I would need a king's ransom to purchase your interests."

"Then, I suppose we shall meet in London on Christmas Eve," replied the deep voice.

"And Portis," Mull asked, "do you agree with the rest?"

Uncle Portis replied in a measured voice. "This is not of my doing. While I may disagree with Treemont and the others, it is their right to act as they deem appropriate. However, I do not believe that the clause should be invoked without some reasonable opportunity to correct the problem."

"Nonsense!" the deep voice boomed. "He has had his chances. I've raised concerns over the last year about Brogdon Honeycutt and whether we were doing everything we could to sign him. It was not a surprise that he went elsewhere."

"His demands were absurd," interjected Mull.

"His demands were those of an eccentric author whose next book will sell millions of copies and will be made into a movie. His demands could have been met," insisted Treemont.

"Enough!" interrupted Uncle Portis. The room fell silent. "I hope no one in this room would seek to invoke the clause without adequate justification and warning."

Once again there was a general murmur of agreement from the group.

"So we are in agreement that Mull should be offered a fair chance. But what does that mean? The clause was intended to be exercised when the owner of the business was incapable of operating it. Sales alone are not and have never been a sufficient reason."

"Then what is a good enough reason?" demanded

Treemont. "What must we do to get this ship straight?"

"I am not sure," replied Uncle Portis.

Colophon chanced another peek around the vase. Her father was sitting in one of the large leather chairs in the middle of the room. Opposite him, Treemont was sitting in another. The rest of the family hovered throughout the library. Colophon quickly withdrew back into her hiding spot.

After much mumbling by and between the family members, Mull, who had sat silent for this period, finally spoke: "I have a proposal."

Treemont hushed the rest and turned to Mull. "Go ahead," he said in his deep voice.

"Give me until our meeting on Christmas Eve. I'm scheduled to meet with three authors over the course of the next month to discuss long-term publishing contracts. A book deal of three or more books from any of these authors would be more than enough to guarantee the financial stability of this company for the next decade and beyond."

"Who are the authors?" Treemont demanded.

"Roger Scornsbury, Natasha Limekicker, and Pat O'Dally," replied Mull. "Scornsbury is coming into town in a couple of weeks to discuss a publishing deal. If I can get that deal completed, all of the prior problems will be behind us."

No one immediately spoke. Peering around the corner of the vase, Colophon could see from the look on Treemont's face that her father's offer had taken him by surprise. She was not sure if her father actually had meetings arranged with those authors, or if he was bluffing.

Uncle Portis spoke. "I assume the signing of a contract of three or more books with an established, best-selling author would suffice?"

There was yet another murmur of concurrence from those in the room.

"Then," continued Uncle Portis, "by December twenty-forth at midnight, if Mull delivers a deal to publish three or more books from a best-selling author, the business is his to run without any further interference from the family. If he fails to deliver, you may vote to invoke the clause, if that remains the will of the family. Are we agreed?"

One by one the members of the family in the room expressed their agreement, with one exception.

"Treemont," Uncle Portis said, "are you in agreement?"

Treemont stood and walked over to the fireplace. "If that is what is required. However, let me be completely clear. If, at the stroke of midnight on December twenty-fourth, the requirement has not been met, there will be no extensions, no excuses, and no second chances."

"Agreed," Uncle Portis replied. "Now, I believe we should all return to the living room before the rest of the family begins to worry about what we are doing in here behind closed doors."

And with that, everyone departed, with the exception of Uncle Portis, who closed the large oak doors behind him and stepped back into the middle of the room. Colophon, who had been crouching behind the vase for almost half an hour, wondered if she would ever be able to leave.

"Colophon, you may come out from behind the vase now," Uncle Portis said.

Colophon froze and held her breath. Surely he had not said what she thought he just said.

"Come now, girl, I don't have all night."

There was no escape. "How . . . ?" Colophon said as she stood and tried to stretch the cramps out of her legs.

"Oh, you can't be serious. You made enough noise to wake the dead. The problem was that everyone else was so busy arguing that they wouldn't have heard a train plow through the front door. I, however, am an editor. My job is to pay attention to the details. And a detail you were. So come down here and join me."

Colophon descended the circular staircase and stood before Uncle Portis. "How could you?" she demanded.

He pointed to the large leather chair next to him. Colophon sat down and sank deep into it. Uncle Portis appeared to have aged ten years since dinner.

"I trust you understand what just happened?"

Colophon fidgeted in the leather chair. "I think so."

"There was no choice, dear. Technically, the family has the right to do this. However, I convinced the others in private—with the exception of Treemont, of course—that your father deserved the chance to set the business straight."

"But what happened was not his fault," Colophon protested.

"No, it was not. And I argued that very point. Treemont, however, has convinced everyone that there is no one else to blame and that there is no one else who can accept the responsibility. The family is looking to your father as the party responsible for the current state of the business, whether these events could have been prevented or not."

"But I thought they liked my father."

"Oh, but my dear child, they do—again, with the exception of Treemont. Treemont has always been jealous of your father. He was every bit as successful as your father academically and in everything they attempted. But it didn't matter, and Treemont knew that. No matter what he did, no matter how successful or smart he was, the business was going to be turned over to your father. That is, as I'm sure you are painfully aware, the family rule."

Colophon nodded again.

"The family adores your father. However, this is a family business. They want to ensure that the business prospers, not just for their sake, but for the sake of their children and their grandchildren. Treemont has convinced them that your father's ownership of the company has placed that future at risk."

"But how could he have prevented—"

"He could not have. However, that is beside the point. What matters now is perception, not reality. The question is whether the family has confidence in his leadership. Treemont has spent months—perhaps years—undermining that confidence among the other family members."

"What will happen?"

"If your father is not able to meet the terms of the agreement, ownership of the company, and everything that goes along with that ownership, would transfer to the next in line of direct lineage from Miles Letterford's second son."

There was a period of silence. Colophon finally spoke.

"Everything?"

"Everything."

"This house?"

"This house, the home in London—they would be the homes of the new owner."

Again, a long silence.

"Who?"

"I am quite sure you already know the answer to that," replied Uncle Portis.

"Treemont?"

"Yes," said Uncle Portis. "I am afraid that unless your father is able to complete the task he has taken on by the stroke of midnight on Christmas Eve, it will all become Treemont's."

"But can't father purchase the whole company? Didn't Treemont say that?"

"Yes. In theory he could," replied Uncle Portis. "However, Miles Letterford wanted the owner of the majority interest to account to the other owners. Your father would have to pay each of the other three sets of descendants the full value of the company to purchase their interests. There is not a bank in the world that would loan him that amount of money."

Colophon sat still and contemplated what Uncle Portis had said. It sounded so final. Then a thought occurred to her.

"Uncle Portis?"

"Yes, dear?"

"Do you think that everything that has happened has been simply a series of accidents?"

The question seemed to catch Uncle Portis off guard. He sat back in his seat and looked at Colophon. "What do you mean?"

"Well, it seems that a whole lot of bad things happened all at once. Weird things. Would Treemont—"

"Now, now, surely you're not suggesting—"

"I'm just saying that it's mighty strange how everything occurred."

"Young lady, that will be enough of that talk. Treemont may be many things, but I do not believe for a minute that he would do anything intentional to harm this company."

"But—"

"No buts. The only thing you can do now is support your father. He does not need to be distracted by any-thing—particularly unfounded conspiracy theories. He has a task to complete, a difficult one. I suggest you let him focus and do what you can to make his life easy over the next month."

Colophon nodded.

"Good. Now, I understand that there was some pecan pie left over from dinner. Why don't you run down and get some?"

Although she was not in the least bit hungry, Colophon nodded again, stood up and walked out of the room. Uncle Portis, however, stayed in his seat looking very much like he was contemplating Colophon's last question.

Chapter Nine
Quittance or Obligation

Friday, November 28

"Why should I care?" asked Case, displaying little or no interest in his sister's concerns as he flopped onto his bed and started fumbling with his ever-present iPod.

"Case," protested Colophon, "this is serious."

Colophon had just spent fifteen minutes describing to her older brother the conversation she had overheard in the library.

"Like I said, I don't care. It's dad's business, not yours. Not mine."

"You should care. It will be your business one day."

"Please, don't remind me," replied Case.

"You should be proud to run the family business. The family tradition goes back for several—"

"Several centuries, I know. Trust me, I've listened to the stories for more years than you have. How it will one day be my obligation. Blah, blah, blah. My duty to the family. Blah, blah, blah. I would just as soon see the whole business go away."

"You don't mean that!" exclaimed Colophon.

"As a matter of fact, I do." Case turned away from his sister, put in his earbuds, and turned up the volume on his iPod.

Colophon was infuriated. How could her brother turn his back on the family business? All she had ever wanted to do was be part of Letterford & Sons. It meant everything to her. She took a deep breath. She knew that yelling at him wouldn't help. She needed another approach. She walked around the bed and tapped him on the shoulder. He took out his earbuds.

"What?"

"So, tell me—how is Samantha Peet? Brett Haven? Glenn Eldridge? Still hanging out with that crowd?"

"None of your business."

"Nice people, I'm sure. And they all come from very wealthy families. Isn't Samantha's father the CEO of something or other?"

Case turned off his iPod and stared at his sister.

"What's your point?" he asked suspiciously.

"The point is that you hang out with a bunch of rich snobs."

"They are not a bunch of—"

"Oh, spare me," replied Colophon. "They wouldn't even talk to you if your father were not the owner of a world-famous publishing house."

"That's not true."

"Really? You know as well as I do that your little group consists of nothing but spoiled rich kids who look down on anyone who was not born with a silver spoon in their mouth."

"Whatever," said Case. "You're just jealous."

"Fine—they are wonderful, caring people. But tell me something. How will Samantha and the rest of your snobby friends react when your father is thrown from his position in the company, stripped of his business, and kicked out of his house? It will be on the front page of every business paper on this planet."

Case started to say something, then paused. Finally he replied halfheartedly: "Samantha and my friends don't care about that."

"I'm sure they don't. They seem to be a very understanding group." She stood by the door and stared at her brother.

Case started to protest but fell silent. He walked over to the window in his room that overlooked the front lawn." There's nothing we can do, you know. Dad is either going to get the contract or he won't. We can't help."

"Case," Colophon said, "I don't think what happened to those other authors were accidents."

Case turned to face his sister. "What do you mean?"

"It's just too much of a coincidence. All those things happened all at once, and then this Treemont guy shows up."

"Oh, c'mon," responded Case. "You don't really think—"

"Case, you didn't hear this man. You didn't see his eyes. I think he would be willing to do anything. Think about it. He would get everything. Everything."

"Even if he did have something to do with what happened—and I'm not saying he did—the point is, what can we do? Nothing, that's what. Nothing."

"Dad will be meeting soon with the first author. At the very least, you could tag along and keep an eye on things."

"So I just go up to Dad and tell him I want to tag along when he meets with this author? I'm so sure that plan is going to work."

"Just ask," replied Colophon. "At least try. But

don't tell Dad what you're doing. We're not supposed to know what's going on. He would freak out if he knew that we knew."

Case contemplated simply ignoring his sister's request. But what if something did happen and he could have helped? Colophon wouldn't shut up about it for the rest of his life. "Fine," Case finally said. "I'll try to do something, and I'll keep it a secret. I still think you're crazy, though. And by the way, what will you be doing while I'm saving Dad?"

"I have a mystery to solve," replied Colophon.

Chapter Ten
Most Ponderous and
Substantial Things

Saturday, November 29
8:15 p.m.

Colophon lay on her back near the old persimmon tree at the edge of the field and stared up at the night sky. Maggie, the family's golden retriever, snuggled up warmly against her side. The night air was cool, but the ground still retained remnants of the summer heat. A light sweater and a warm golden retriever proved more than sufficient to keep her comfortable.

Far from the lights that infested the cities and the suburbs on a 24/7 basis, the night sky over the Letterford property was actually dark. And on those occasions when the moon was absent from the sky (a night just such as this), the sky was filled with an unimaginable number of stars. On her back in the field, Colophon looked up at the delicate pinpoints of light set against a deep pool of black. Case had his iPod to escape from the world; Colophon had the stars.

Maggie stirred momentarily, let out a halfhearted growl, and fell immediately back to sleep. Colophon turned her head and discovered that her father was now standing by her side.

"Hi, Dad."

"Hi, honey," replied Mull Letterford. "Isn't it a bit cool to be outside on the ground?"

"I needed a break."

Mull sat down by his daughter. "I know exactly what you mean." He sounded exhausted.

"Dad?"

"Yes?"

"Is there really a Letterford family treasure?"

"Besides yourself?"

"Seriously, Dad. Is there a family treasure?"

"You've been talking with Julian, haven't you?"

"Yes, but—"

"Julian is a fine man, a very intelligent man. He could have been a very important part of the family business, but he has spent years obsessing over this so-called family treasure. It has ruined his life."

"So you don't believe in the treasure?"

"Belief is immaterial," replied Mull. "Whether I believe or don't believe changes nothing. It either exists or it doesn't. I would love to believe a treasure exists. As a child I listened to the same stories as Julian, and I desperately wanted to believe in the treasure. But that was all it was—a belief. Not fact. Not reality. And belief was not enough. So I grew up and put that behind me. Julian didn't."

"But," asked Colophon, "he seems so . . . certain."

"His belief oppresses him."

Colophon stared up at the night sky in silence.

"I shouldn't be so harsh in my judgment of Julian," said Mull. "It's just that—well . . . I just don't have a lot of room for false hope right now."

Colophon wanted desperately to tell her father that she had overheard the conversation in the library, that she knew exactly what he was going through. She wanted to tell him that there was still hope, and that she believed in him. But she couldn't. And so they sat in the field in silence together and watched the stars make their way across the night sky.

CHAPTER ELEVEN
Use Careful Watch;
Choose Trusty Sentinels

Warm Springs, Georgia
Sunday, December 14

Old maps of the state of Georgia show a small
town by the name of Bullochville, located just a

few short miles to the northwest of Manchester at the base of Georgia's Pine Mountain. Founded by a family of local merchants in the nineteenth century, the small southern city became known for the warm—not hot—natural spring that percolates up through the mountain. The waters from the spring were long believed to have restorative abilities. This very belief led the future president Franklin Delano Roosevelt, who suffered from polio, to the town in 1924. Significantly—and perhaps not coincidently—the town changed its name to Warm Springs that same year. The water flowing forth from the spring brought Roosevelt back to his small cottage in Warm Springs for the rest of his life. In fact, Roosevelt ultimately passed away in 1945 at that small cottage. The town, for all practical purposes, remains much as it appeared when Franklin Delano Roosevelt was its most famous part-time citizen.

It is, literally, a one-stoplight town. It consists of two rows of buildings built in the late nineteenth century which contain a variety of shops, restaurants, and a small hotel—the Warm Springs Inn —all separated by the wide expanse (but limited length) of Broad Street. The Warm Springs Inn, a narrow three-story building, sits on the north side of Broad Street and is adjacent to the abandoned railroad tracks that once brought visitors to the town from far and wide.

The meeting between Mull Letterford and Roger Scornsbury was scheduled to take place over lunch at the inn. Contrary to Colophon's suggestion, her father expressed no interest in permitting his fifteen-year-old son to accompany him to the most important business meeting of his life. Fortunately, it was not uncommon for the Letterford children to visit the small town, particularly as it was just a short bike ride from the Letterford property. As Colophon pointed out to her brother, their father did not want Case to accompany him to the lunch meeting, but he had not specifically forbidden Case from visiting Warm Springs that day.

After returning home from church, Case changed quickly into a pair of jeans and a T-shirt, threw on a denim jacket, and headed to the garage, where he kept his bike. An abandoned railroad bed ran all the way from the rear of the Letterford property into downtown Warm Springs. It was, in fact, the same track on which President Roosevelt had once traveled from Washington, D.C. Case watched from the garage and waited until his father had left the house before he headed to the railroad bed. On his bike, Case could get to the town in around fifteen minutes, much faster than his father could navigate through the countryside by car.

Case arrived on the outskirts of town and parked his bike in the woods. He carefully made his way to a small access road at the rear of the buildings lining Broad Street and then down a narrow alley to a coffee shop located across the street from the Warm Springs Inn. A bell on the door rang as Case slipped into the shop.

"Afternoon, Case," said Annette Parker, the owner. "What brings you into town today?"

Annette was a petite woman in her midfifties with short-cropped salt-and-pepper hair. She always wore pink and, despite working in a coffee shop, was always dressed in her Sunday best.

"Nothing much, Ms. Annette," Case replied. "Just hanging out, I suppose."

"Did you come with your father? I hear he has a big meeting today at the inn. Is it something important? A big author? I'll bet it's something really exciting. Is he here yet? It would be great to meet a famous author. Do you know who it is?"

The words shot out at Case in rapid succession.

Case wasn't surprised that Annette Parker knew about his father's meeting. In a small town such as Warm Springs, everybody knows your business.

"I think he does have a meeting. But I really don't know what it's about. I just wanted to get out of the house for a while."

"I understand completely," she replied. "Sometimes you just need some fresh air. Great day, don't you think? Nice and sunny, but cool, just like November should be. I hate it when November is warm, don't you? Ruins the whole feel of the season. People certainly drink more coffee when it's cold, I can tell you that. Although more people are drinking iced coffee than I have ever seen before. Didn't see that five years ago. Coffee was hot, not cold. But hey, no skin off my back. If they want it cold, I'll give it to them cold. So, what can I get you? The usual—black cherry soda? You really need to try a scone. I made them fresh this morning. Nothing better than a fresh scone."

Case purchased a black cherry soda and a cinnamon chip scone and then took a seat at the front of the shop. From his vantage point, he could see the front door of the Warm Springs Inn. Fortunately, another customer had arrived to draw Annette's attention. Case sat back, sipped his soda, and waited for his father to arrive.

Chapter Twelve
A Good Direction

Notwithstanding her father's lack of belief in the treasure, Colophon began formulating a plan to track it down. She decided that she first needed to narrow her search.

Miles Letterford had lived his entire life on the other side of the Atlantic and never set foot on North American soil. It seemed unlikely to Colophon that the treasure would be found in America.

From her perspective, that same logic effectively eliminated every continent but Europe. Sure, a clue or two (such as the portrait) might have been transported to this country, but it seemed unlikely that the treasure itself would have made its way over the ocean—not without being inadvertently discovered at some point.

All right, so I have narrowed it down to one continent, she thought. *For what that's worth.*

Colophon, however, also believed that Miles Letterford would not have placed the treasure in a location where it could be easily moved, as such an occurrence would have rendered all his well-laid clues meaningless. No, he would have placed the treasure in a well-hidden spot, but in an area that he knew. An area that he was comfortable with.

The treasure, she determined, *must be in England.* And with that, Colophon decided, England was where she needed to go.

Getting to England actually proved to be the easiest part of the plan. The family always celebrated Christmas at their home in London. Meg Letterford would leave for London that very afternoon to begin preparations. It was not a particularly odd request on Colophon's part to accompany her mother to London—she had certainly done so in the past over the holidays. She asked her father, and he said yes.

Colophon knew that at least one significant clue was located in America—the portrait of Miles

Letterford. Obviously, she was not going to be permitted to simply pack it up and take it with her to London. Digital photos would have to do. She turned on all the lights in the foyer and stood in front of the portrait on the stool from the library. She took a picture of the entire painting, and then, moving section by section around it, she took close-up photographs in an effort to capture every detail. As a precaution, she also took photographs of the frame, as it bore the first clue—the rhyme. Returning to her room, Colophon downloaded the photos to her notebook computer and ran off a copy of each picture, which she placed in a small folder that she intended to carry with her to London.

CHAPTER THIRTEEN
All Strange and Terrible Events

Case sipped his soda as his father's car turned down Broad Street and parked in front of the hotel. Mull Letterford stepped from his car and glanced up and down the sidewalk. As of yet, there was no sign of Roger Scornsbury. Mull checked his watch, took one last glance down the sidewalk, and then headed into the hotel lobby and out of Case's view.

The previous evening Case had asked his father

about the meeting and Scornsbury. The question, coming from Case (who normally expressed absolutely no interest in the family's business), surprised his father. Nonetheless, he explained to Case that Scornsbury was a famous author who lived in Atlanta. Although he considered Scornsbury a nice enough fellow, Mull Letterford expressed some concern over the meeting because of Scornsbury's peculiarities.

"What peculiarities?" asked Case.

"You see," replied Mull, "Scornsbury is a very talented writer—very talented. However, he suffers from globophobia."

"Globophobia?"

"Yes, globophobia—an extreme fear of balloons."

Case had laughed. "Balloons?"

"Yes, balloons. And it's not funny. Apparently it developed after a rather bad incident at a birthday party when he was young. I suggested we meet at his home, but Scornsbury insisted on having breakfast in town at the inn. Fortunately, the owners of the inn have assured me that the dining room is and shall remain balloon free. If all goes well, Scornsbury will be signed to a contract before the final cup of coffee is poured."

All, however, did not go well.

✦ ✦ ✦

Mull Letterford sat in the inn's dining room and sipped his coffee as he waited for his guest to arrive. Just as he had been surprised the previous night by his son's sudden interest in the affairs of the company, he was equally surprised by his daughter's request to accompany her mother to London. Colophon had always enjoyed staying in Manchester and exploring the countryside. But Mull had no reason for insisting that his daughter stay here. In fact, he thought (somewhat guiltily) that there would be fewer distractions with Colophon and her mother gone. The business he needed to attend to was of the utmost importance. The fewer distractions, the better.

As Mull completed his thought, he noticed the tall lanky figure of Roger Scornsbury walk past the front window and toward the front door of the inn. Seconds later he entered the dining room.

Scornsbury was approximately fifty years old and stood several inches above six feet in height. He towered over Mull Letterford. Scornsbury wore, as was his custom, a three-piece suit. However, as was equally his custom, neither the pants, the coat, nor the vest came from the same ensemble or bore any resemblance in color or pattern. Remarkably, even his shirt and tie were mismatched.

Scornsbury extended his right hand. "Mull Letterford, how are you?"

"Quite well, Roger, and you?"

"Ah, quite the same, quite the same."

Whether "the same" was good, bad, or otherwise was unclear to Mull. Mull gestured toward the open seat, and Scornsbury sat down.

Mull Letterford and Roger Scornsbury had actually known each other for several years, as they were both well-known figures in the publishing industry. Until recently, Scornsbury had been under contract with a large New York City publishing house. However, that relationship had fallen apart in a nasty dispute over the proper use of semicolons. Fortunately, the timing of Scornsbury's departure from his old publishing house had worked out perfectly for Mull.

"So, Mull Letterford, tell me—what would an esteemed publisher such as yourself want with a simple wordsmith such as myself?"

Mull Letterford laughed and launched into his sales pitch.

Case had waited until Scornsbury entered the Warm Springs Inn before leaving the coffee shop and quietly slipping across the street and taking a seat in the inn's lobby. From his vantage point, Case could see his father's back and look directly into the face of Roger Scornsbury. Unfortunately, he was too far away from his father's table to hear what was being said.

What am I doing here? Case thought. His sister was crazy—no one was out to get their father. There was no grand conspiracy. No bad guy. He had to admit, though, that his father had seemed distracted lately. And he seemed tired. Case knew Colophon didn't think he noticed things like that, but he did. And although he would never admit it to his sister, it concerned him.

The reception desk for the hotel, located immediately to Case's right, was staffed by a middle-aged lady with bright red hair. As Case sat watching his father and Scornsbury discuss whatever it was they were discussing, he noticed a man enter the lobby and approach the reception desk. Case, bored with watching his father, turned his attention to the discussion between the man and the receptionist. The two spoke briefly and then walked into the office behind the reception desk.

The door to the hotel opened once again, and to Case's horror, a young woman entered carrying a large collection of balloons.

She's probably delivering the balloons to someone's room, he thought. No need to panic.

The young woman, however, did not head toward the front desk; rather, she headed straight for the dining room. Case shot up from his seat and stood right in front of the delivery girl just as she was set to turn the corner into the dining room.

"Can I help you?" he asked.

The girl looked up at the balloons and then at Case. "I have a balloon delivery."

"Balloons. You have balloons!"

The delivery girl looked at Case, back up at the balloons, and then back at Case. "Yes, I have balloons. I thought I made that clear. The balloons in my hand should have been a dead giveaway. I deliver balloons for a living. That is why my shirt says 'Balloons R Us.' That is why I drive a van with big words on the side that spell 'Balloons R Us.' That is why I have all these balloons in my hand."

Case started to speak when he noticed yet another delivery person walking through the door of the hotel, carrying yet another handful of balloons. And behind that delivery person stood yet another delivery person, who carried yet another handful of balloons.

"Listen, there has been some sort of mistake," Case said to the first delivery girl.

The delivery girl looked at the card on the balloons. "Unless your name is Roger Scornsbury, then these balloons are not for you, and there has been no mistake. Now, please get out of my way."

"I can't let you go in—" Case started to say, but it was too late. The delivery girl turned the corner into the dining room, followed closely behind by the other two deliveries of balloons. All told, a total of twenty-eight balloons entered the room.

Mull Letterford was well into his explanation of why Letterford & Sons was the perfect publishing house for Roger Scornsbury—which he felt was going exceptionally well—when he noticed that Scornsbury's face had gone completely white and his left eye had started to twitch.

"Roger, are you OK? Is something wrong?"

"Balla balla balla," Roger Scornsbury stammered.

"I'm sorry? Is something the matter?"

The twitching got worse. Scornsbury's nontwitching eye grew wide in terror.

"Balla balla balla," Scornsbury repeated.

From the corner of his eye, Mull Letterford saw brief flashes of red, green, blue, and yellow. Balloons filled the space around the table.

"Are you Roger Scornsbury?" the first delivery girl asked.

Scornsbury did not answer. Instead, he bolted upright and ran out of the restaurant. A second later Mull heard the door to the inn slam shut. Immediately after that, Mull saw the terrified face of Roger Scornsbury running down the sidewalk and away from the hotel.

Mull slumped in his chair. The three delivery persons simply stared at him.

"Are you—?" the first delivery girl started to ask again.

"No, my dear girl, I am not Roger Scornsbury," replied Mull. "The gentleman that just left the restaurant was Mr. Scornsbury."

"Odd bird, isn't he," the delivery girl said to no one in particular.

"Yes," Mull replied dejectedly, "odd indeed."

CHAPTER FOURTEEN
Tedious Stumbling Blocks

Colophon received the text message from her brother just minutes before she boarded the plane with her mother. She grimaced as she read it.

"Something the matter, dear?" her mother asked.

"No," Colophon replied, "just something from Case."

Meg Letterford pursed her lips but did not pursue the line of inquiry. Shortly thereafter Colophon and Meg boarded the plane and took their seats. Within minutes Meg fell into a deep sleep.

But Colophon couldn't sleep. She was now convinced that someone was sabotaging her father's efforts. She realized, though, that there was little she could do about it from London. That was up to her brother, which did not exactly ease her mind. Her focus had to be on solving the family mystery. With that thought, she opened her folder and pulled out the photos of the painting. For half an hour, she stared intently at each photograph.

She stared at each detail in the painting.

She stared at a photograph of the entire painting.

She turned it upside down and stared at it sideways.

She hoped something would jump out at her.

Nothing did.

She spent another hour rearranging the letters from the type set—R, G, E, N, D, I, R, H, R, E—into numerous configurations.

DEN HERR RIG

OK, that made a lot of sense.

HERD ERR GIN

Wonderful. She was really getting somewhere now.

END HERR RIG

Oh, c'mon.

GRIND HE ERR

Definitely no.

And then after numerous more nonsensical phrases:

RED HERRING

You have got to be kidding, Colophon thought. Red herring! She had literally spent an hour chasing a red herring!

She stared at the words on her pad. Well, at least she knew the clue wasn't the type set.

She put the pictures on the seat tray in front of her and sat back in her seat. What was she missing?

She pushed the button on the side of her seat and eased it back. She stared up at the ceiling of the plane and thought about the poem on the frame of Miles Letterford's portrait.

> *Good friend among the stars be found,*
> *A treasure — heare the key thus bound.*
> *Blesed be the man who lays the claime*
> *To that encloased within this frame.*

✛ ✛ ✛

Case took the path along the old railroad bed back to the house and was waiting in the kitchen when his father arrived home from the meeting with Roger Scornsbury. He heard his father enter the house and walk down the hallway to his office. Carefully, Case made his way down the hallway — in his socks so as to avoid any noise — and listened outside the door. Inside, he could hear his father speaking on the phone.

"Yes, that's right," Mull said in a depressed voice. "Balloons. And not just one or two, mind you. It seemed as if there were a thousand."

Case crept a little closer to the door.

"No, the next meeting is scheduled for Wednesday in New York. O'Dally is a pain, that's for sure, but at least he won't run screaming from the meeting."

There was a pause, and then a short laugh from Mull Letterford.

"Yes, yes, I will be there fifteen minutes early, perhaps thirty. I know how he feels about punctuality. Anyway, I'll let you know how it goes. Please give my love to Aunt Judith. Yes, thank you."

The receiver clicked down in the phone.

Case silently made his way back down the hallway to the kitchen, where he proceeded to send a text message to his sister describing the conversation he had just overheard. After sending the message, Case headed for the refrigerator, when almost immediately his phone beeped. It was a message back from Colophon: "Go to NY with dad."

Case started to text his sister to tell her that it would be a useless endeavor, even if his father were willing to take him along, which he doubted he would. However, Case quickly realized that such a message would do little good and would result in a never-ending torrent of text messages from across the Atlantic. It would be far easier to simply ask his father if he could go to New York.

The problem was that he could not think of any reason why his father would feel the need to take him to New York, especially on a trip of such importance.

Chapter Fifteen
By the Progress of the Stars

London
Monday, December 15

Colophon arrived at the family's home in London midafternoon. Although she was exhausted, she set up her laptop and pulled up a photo of the painting. She stared at the photo. She zoomed in. She zoomed out. She rotated it counterclockwise and clockwise.

Nothing.

But it must be here somewhere.

The painting, however, did not speak to Colophon. It revealed nothing.

For the remainder of the afternoon, she Googled every object in the painting in conjunction with the term *Letterford* to see if any obvious connections turned up.

Nothing.

She reversed the image.

Nothing.

She converted it to black and white to see if any patterns emerged.

Nothing.

She stared at the painting.

Nothing. Again.

She recited the poem on the frame to herself:

> *"Good friend among the stars be found,*
> *A treasure—heare the key thus bound.*
> *Blesed be the man who lays the claime*
> *To that encloased within this frame."*

Colophon sat upright.

What was enclosed within the frame?

She had not been looking within the frame. She had been looking in the *painting*.

C'mon, Colophon thought. *It couldn't be that simple.*

Could it?

She zoomed in on the medallion on the top right corner of the frame. Inside the medallion was the profile of a man. Under the man's profile was the name *Nestor.* Around the outer edge of the medallion was a series of stars.

Good friend among the stars be found!

Colophon zoomed over to the medallion on the opposite side of the frame. Another man's profile. And more stars. The medallion identified this man as *Virgil.* The third medallion was located at the bottom of the frame. This man had a full beard, was slightly balding, and, to be quite honest, was not particularly handsome. Colophon, however, instantly recognized the name under this medallion: *Socrates.* Again, the medallion was circled by stars.

Among the stars be found—a treasure!

Socrates.

Nestor.

Virgil.

This had to be the clue that Cousin Julian had been looking for all these years. Colophon Googled each name in turn. Nestor, it turned out, was the king of Pylus and considered the wisest of the Greek kings. Virgil was a famous Roman poet. Socrates was a famous Greek philosopher.

But what's their connection?

Colophon stared at the screen of her laptop.

Great, she thought, *I am now officially in over my head.*

Case spent most of the day thinking of how he could convince his father to take him to New York. As he prepared to enter his father's office to make his pitch, he took a deep breath and knocked.

"Dad, do you have a second?"

"Anytime," replied Mull, "You know that. Come on in."

Case entered his father's office and sat in one of the chairs in front the desk. Again, he took a deep breath.

"I have a research paper due when I get back to school after the holidays."

This was a true statement.

"I've decided to write about a dinosaur from the late Jurassic period—the Apatosaurus."

Not true. Plain old lie. His paper was due in social studies.

"I've been doing a lot of research on the Apato-saurus—"

Absolutely not true. Lightning was sure to strike at any moment.

"—however, I would really like to see the fossil of an Apatosaurus in person. I think it would help my paper. It turns out that the best specimen in America is located at the American Museum of Natural History in New York City."

True, at least according to the museum's website.

"Anyway, if you were going to New York City any-time soon I'd like to tag along so that I can go to the museum."

Mull Letterford looked across the desk at his son. "I'm leaving for New York first thing in the morning. Audrey was going to come down for a couple of days to watch over things, but if you want to join me, that's fine. Just remember, I have an important meeting to attend tomorrow, so you'll need to go to the museum by yourself."

Case tried to hide his surprise at how easy it had been to convince his father. "Oh, that's . . . uh, great. Thanks."

"I'm heading out the door at nine-thirty. Don't be late, or you'll be stuck here at home."

Case was already heading toward the door.

"Got it—nine-thirty in the morning. I'll be ready."

Case stepped into the hallway, pulled the door shut, and headed for his room. As he walked, he texted his sister: "Going to NYC. I better not be wasting my time."

CHAPTER SIXTEEN
A Secret to Reveal

London
Tuesday, December 16
8:45 a.m.

Colophon ran off several photos of the frame and headed downstairs to the kitchen. As she reached the bottom of the stairs, she heard her mother engaged in conversation with someone whose voice sounded particularly familiar, although the name matching the voice did not immediately come to mind. As she turned in to the kitchen, the familiar voice spoke once more: "Well, of course, Margaret, Tuttlenewt was completely wrong in his assumptions about— Colophon! How are you dear girl?"

"Julian!" Colophon exclaimed as she rushed forward to greet her recently discovered relative. "What are you doing here?"

"Now, Coly," said Meg, "is that any way to speak to Julian?"

"Meg, its fine, really," replied Julian, leaping to Colophon's defense. "The girl was simply taken by surprise. I'm sure that she didn't expect to see me sitting in her kitchen this morning." He turned to Colophon. "I am, as usual, chasing yet another clue to the treasure. I understand that there is a wonderful seventeenth-century book on secret codes at the British Library. I thought I would spend some time tomorrow poring over it."

"Well," Meg replied, "that's for tomorrow. As for today, please see to it that Colophon minds her manners while I am gone."

"Gone? Are you going somewhere this morning?" asked Colophon.

"Not a bit of groceries in the house. I imagine

you will want to eat at some point. Anyway, Julian has graciously agreed to hang around and keep you company."

"Mom, you know I'm old enough—"

"I know," replied Meg, "but—"

"I'm still your little girl."

"And always will be." Colophon's mother grabbed her purse and opened the door. "I'll be back in an hour or so. Call me if you need anything." The bell over the door to the kitchen jingled as she departed.

Before Julian could utter a word, Colophon blurted out: "The painting is not the clue!"

"Excuse me?"

"The painting is not the clue!"

"Why, of course it is. I simply haven't figured out what it means."

"No, no, no. Think about the rhyme. The key is in the frame . . . IN THE FRAME. That doesn't mean in the picture. It means the frame itself."

"That's absurd," Julian protested. "Why, it doesn't even—"

Colophon interrupted, "Think about it. The first line of the poem—'among the stars are found.' Each of the medallions on the frame is surrounded by stars. Stars." She handed Julian a blow-up of each medallion.

"Well, this certainly doesn't prove—"

He paused midsentence and looked down at his coffee.

"I have to go."

"But I thought my mom wanted you to stay with me?"

He stood up and looked around the kitchen. "I really must go. Have you seen my jacket? I'm afraid I've misplaced my jacket." His voice was uneven.

"What's the matter?" Colophon asked.

"Nothing is the matter," he replied with a catch in his voice. "Nothing. Nothing at all. I'll get my coat later. I have to leave." He opened the door. The bell tingled.

"Did I do something wrong?" Colophon asked. "Maybe I'm wrong. Maybe it isn't the frame."

Julian stopped with his back to Colophon—the door slightly ajar. "No, you are right. You are precisely correct. It's just not easy realizing that you spent the majority of your life looking down the wrong path. I simply cannot face that right now."

"But you weren't wasting your time. If you were wasting your time, you never would have shown up at Thanksgiving dinner. We wouldn't have met that day. We wouldn't have looked at the painting together. I wouldn't be sitting here today having this conversation with you."

"I'm sorry," Julian said as he let the door shut behind him.

"But I can't figure out what the clue means!" Colophon shouted at the door. "I need your help!"

There was no response. Colophon sat down and stared at the photos on the table. She felt like she was going to cry. Now she would never be able to find the treasure. And her only other hope rested on her brother—the selfish, inconsiderate jerk who didn't care about anyone but himself.

Her father's business was doomed.

The bell on the kitchen door tingled again. The door opened, and in walked Julian.

"Well, let's hear what you have," he said as he walked over to the kitchen table. "Wasted enough time as it is. No sense wasting any more."

"Julian!" Colophon exclaimed as she stood up and threw her arms around him.

"C'mon, c'mon, I don't have time for this touchy-feely stuff," he responded. "Let's get to work."

"One question before we start."

"Very well," he replied. "If you insist."

"Why did you come back inside?"

Julian wiped his eyes with a handkerchief. "Please don't misunderstand me. This caught me off guard. I've searched for years for this clue, and then in no time at all, you uncover it. A twelve-year-old girl no less. No offense."

"None taken," Colophon said, although it did offend her. She wished people would quit mentioning her age.

"So there I am—standing outside the kitchen door feeling sorry for myself. And then it hit me."

"What?"

"I realized that you may have just proved everything I believe. After all the years of being the butt of so many jokes among members of our family, my belief in the treasure may finally be validated."

"Well then," Colophon said, "I guess it's time to figure out what this means."

Julian stood up straight and composed himself. "Indeed."

Colophon carefully reviewed for Cousin Julian everything she had discovered in the frame. She handed him the research she had run off on each of the figures represented in the frame.

"Nestor, Virgil, and Socrates," Julian said to no one in particular.

"Yes," Colophon replied, "but I can't figure out the connection."

"Well, let's try a few more searches and see what turns up," he suggested.

She retrieved her laptop and returned to the kitchen.

"OK," he said, "let's start with the search terms *Nestor* and *Letterford.*"

Colophon entered the search terms and pressed enter.

"Nothing."

Undeterred, Julian suggested the terms *Socrates* and *Letterford.* Again nothing. Next came the terms *Virgil* and *Letterford.* Nothing. Again.

"See," Colophon exclaimed, "nothing. I can't find a connection with Miles Letterford."

Cousin Julian stared out the kitchen window in thought. "Perhaps," he finally said, "the connection is not with Letterford."

"What do you mean? It's a clue, isn't it?"

"Of that I am quite sure," Julian said. "However, the question is what the clue is intended to lead us to. It may not be the treasure at all. It may simply lead to another clue."

"OK, then where do we go from here?"

"Let's see what the connection is between Nestor, Socrates, and Virgil."

Colophon entered the search terms and pressed enter. She and Julian gasped when they saw the search results.

The first search result simply read: "Nestor-Socrates-Virgil. The first two lines (in Latin) of the inscription on the Shakespeare Monument at Stratford-upon-Avon . . ."

"Remarkable," exclaimed Julian as he sat back in his chair.

"It can't be a coincidence, can it?" asked Colophon.

"Hardly. That must be the next clue—the monument."

"So what do we do now?"

"Now," answered Cousin Julian with an energy heretofore lacking in his demeanor, "now, we take a field trip!"

Manchester, Georgia
Tuesday, December 16
9:30 a.m.

Case was waiting downstairs in the foyer for his father, his bag packed and ready to go. This seemed to catch Mull Letterford off guard.

"I thought I was going to have to track you down," he said.

"I guess I'm just excited about getting to New York," replied Case.

Mull Letterford eyed his son suspiciously. Rather than risk further inquiry, Case grabbed his laptop and headed toward the front door.

"C'mon, Dad. Need to get going. Don't want to miss our plane."

Mull Letterford, who had far greater issues to deal with than his son's apparent change in attitude (albeit a positive change), simply shrugged, grabbed his leather folder, and followed his son outside to the waiting car.

Palace Hotel, room 723
New York City
Tuesday, December 16
9:32 p.m.

Case bit into his hamburger, closed his eyes, and savored the experience.

Perfect.

Room service—a hamburger, fries, and a Coke.

And TV.

While lying in bed.

Perfect.

Mull Letterford cleared his throat.

Case opened his eyes and looked at his father, who now stood between him and the TV.

"OK, before I lose you completely to the TV and your meal, let's discuss tomorrow. Here's the plan. My meeting is at eleven-thirty, about three blocks from the Natural History Museum. I'll be having lunch at a restaurant with Mr. O'Dally. I'll drop you off at the museum around nine a.m. and then head over to my meeting. I'll be back to pick you up at one-thirty outside the museum."

Case wiped ketchup from his face. "If it's only three blocks away, then why are you dropping me off so early? The museum may not even open until ten."

"I'm sorry, but O'Dally is an absolute stickler for punctuality. I don't intend to be late."

"But two hours early? C'mon Dad, what would he do if you were five minutes late? Is he going to refuse to speak with you?"

"Actually, yes—he would refuse to speak with me. Writers are . . . peculiar. You'd better learn that now. They live in their own unique universes. With O'Dally, a second late may as well be a day late. He is a neat freak, a punctuality freak, and he demands the same of everyone in his life. He has his breakfast served at exactly the same time each day—7:57 a.m. Not 7:58. Not 7:56. It must be 7:57 a.m. exactly—at the exact same diner, sitting at the exact same table every single day. Lunch and dinner are served in equally precise fashion. His life is regimented down to the minute. And so yes, he would refuse to speak with me."

Case started to press the issue when two knocks on their door interrupted the discussion.

Mull opened the door. "Yes, may I help you?"

A short stocky man in a hotel uniform stood outside the door. "Good evening Mr. Letterford. I'm Rupert, the floor valet. I'm here to pick up your shoes."

"Wonderful—hold on just a second." Mull walked over to the bathroom and retrieved the shoes, which he had placed in a plastic bag.

"Are you sure that they'll be ready by the morning?"

"Oh yes," replied Rupert the valet. "In fact, I'll see to it personally and have them back to your room within an hour."

Mull handed the valet a five-dollar tip. "Thank you so much. You're a real lifesaver."

"The pleasure's all mine," replied Rupert.

✢ ✢ ✢

The door to the room shut.

Five dollars? Rupert crammed the five-dollar bill in his pocket. *Give me a break.*

He started down the hallway. When he reached the elevators, he turned and looked back to ensure that no one else was in the corridor. Then, instead of heading downstairs in the elevator to polish the shoes, he walked down the corridor and took the stairs up to the next floor. Exiting onto the eighth floor, he looked around and, seeing no one, quickly knocked on the door of the room directly opposite the entrance to the stairs. The door cracked open ever so slightly.

"Here are the shoes," said the valet.

A hand reached out and grabbed the shoes. A second later a hundred-dollar bill appeared in the crack of the door.

The valet grabbed the bill.

"Hey," said the valet, "you promised me five hundred dollars to deliver the shoes."

A deep voice from behind the door replied: "And when you deliver the shoes back to Mr. Letterford, you will get the remainder. I don't want you to back out on me."

"I wouldn't chicken out."

"Yes," the voice replied, "you would. Be back here in thirty minutes. The shoes will be waiting on you."

The door shut. The valet crammed the hundred-dollar bill into his pocket, checked his watch, and then proceeded back down the hall to the elevator.

CHAPTER EIGHTEEN
The Insolent Foe

Palace Hotel, room 812
Tuesday, December 16

"How did you know my cousin would get a shoe shine?" asked Treemont.

"It's my job to know," replied Trigue James. He did not offer any further explanation.

Best to let him wonder, James thought.

But, James knew, it was not that impressive at all—just some basic detective work and an understanding of human nature. Treemont had already told him that Mull Letterford *always* stayed at the Palace Hotel. All it took was a couple hundred dollars in the hand of the concierge to find out that Letterford *always* requested a shoe shine. People are creatures of habit. James counted on that.

"Now," James said, "I have to get to work. We don't have much time."

James was of medium height and medium build, dressed neatly—but not overly dressed—and in every conceivable way absolutely average in appearance. He was a decent-looking man but could not be described as handsome. His hair was light brown, and his haircut conservative, but not overly so. He had no facial hair, wore no glasses, and his eyes were some indeterminate mix of brown and light green. He had no tattoos, scars, or distinguishing marks of any kind. He was normal-looking—the type of man who could easily fade into the background at a state fair or state dinner—and it suited his unique profession to be so.

James removed the shoes from the bag and carefully placed them on a towel on the bathroom counter. He then proceeded to clean, buff, and polish them to a high gloss.

He held the shoes up for Treemont to see. "Just like new," he said.

Treemont nodded. It was a professional shine job. He was impressed.

James then took the shoes and placed them on a small desk. He loosened the laces to expose the insole of each shoe. Using a scalpel, he carefully peeled back the insoles and then, with a small plastic bottle, squeezed several lines of a clear gluelike substance on the inside of each shoe. He then made several small holes in the back of each insole with the point of the scalpel and rolled the insoles back down over the gluelike material.

"What is that stuff?" Treemont asked.

James held up the bottle. "This, my friend, is (E)-2-butene-1-thiol and (E)-S-2-butenyl thioacetate. The particles are embedded in an acrylic matrix and then suspended in a gel that hardens into a clear, undetectable substance."

"What does it do? Is it a poison? I told you, I'm not trying to kill him."

"No," replied James, "it's not a poison. That would cost extra."

He paused briefly, as if waiting for Treemont to reply to his not-so-subtle inquiry. Treemont gave no indication that he intended to pursue this more drastic approach.

James continued: "I understand that another approach is required in this particular instance. No, this is not a poison, although I suspect that tomorrow your dear cousin will wish it was. Rather, the chemicals in this small bottle represent a synthesized version of the active ingredients excreted by the *Mephitis mephitis.*"

"A what?" asked Treemont.

James laughed. "A *Mephitis mephitis*—the common striped skunk. It is, in fact, a very refined—and very potent—form of that spray."

"Skunk spray? What are you talking about? I can't smell a thing."

"And you won't, so long as you don't wear the shoes. However, once the shoes are put on, the heat from his feet will slowly activate other substances that will dissolve the acrylic matrix and release the chemicals."

Treemont was unimpressed. "So his shoes will stink. So what? He'll find another pair."

"Hardly. I once forced the evacuation of the entire

United Nations with this simple concoction. These chemicals don't wash off. They can't be scrubbed off. They bond to everything they come in contact with —everything. A skunk's spray is bad enough. This formulation is ten times as potent. Once it activates, there is nothing Mull Letterford will be able to do to get rid of the smell."

"I still don't see how this is going to stop him from getting to the meeting."

James looked at Treemont, smiled, and handed him the shoes. "Patience, good sir. You will see."

Rupert knocked on the door. Truth be told, he *had* given serious consideration to simply walking away and not returning to pick up the shoes. He had no idea what was happening to the shoes he had delivered to this same room.

But honestly, Rupert argued to himself, *exactly what can they do to a pair of shoes? It can't be that bad, can it?*

And besides, money was money, and he needed money.

The door cracked open just wide enough for a bag and four one-hundred-dollar bills to pass through. Rupert tried to catch a quick glance at the face of his unnamed coconspirator, but the door shut quickly.

He held up the bag and looked at the shoes. *Nice shine job,* he thought as he headed back downstairs to return the shoes.

Chapter Nineteen
Heirs of Fixed Destiny

England
Wednesday, December 17

Colophon convinced her mother that a day trip to Stratford-upon-Avon would be an exciting educational experience, and as Julian was willing and available to accompany her, Meg readily agreed. Julian picked her up before sunrise, and they headed north on the M40 motorway.

For most of the journey, Julian and Colophon speculated on what they might find in Stratford-upon-Avon and where the next clue might lead. The conversation was lighthearted and optimistic. A few kilometers from the town, however, Julian abruptly changed the tone of the conversation. "Tell me," he said, "why the interest in the family treasure?"

Colophon stared out the window. "Nothing really, I suppose. Just seems interesting." She saw no need for Julian to know about the ultimatum facing her father.

"Twelve-year-old girls do not get up early in the morning to accompany their scruffy cousin on a trip to an old church for fun. There must be more. As the Bard said, perhaps a secret to confer about?"

"The Bard?"

"William Shakespeare!" replied Julian. "The Bard of Avon! The man we now seek. Honestly—what do they teach you in school?"

Colophon continued to stare out the window. "No secrets. No mystery. The treasure just seems interesting."

"I don't suppose," Julian said, "that it has anything to do with the meeting that will take place on Christmas Eve?"

Colophon whirled in her seat and stared at Julian. "How do you know about that?"

"You forget that I am your father's first cousin. I am a Letterford. I have the right to know." He paused. "You think this will help your father, don't you?"

Colophon turned and stared back out the window. "I just wanted to do *something* to help. I thought he might be able to use the treasure to purchase the company outright. You probably think that's silly."

"No, I do not. No more silly than a man in his early forties chasing an unknown treasure across the English countryside with a twelve-year-old girl as his guide."

"OK then," said Colophon. "Fair is fair. Why are you chasing the treasure? What secrets do you hold?"

"Ah, I set myself up for that one, didn't I? Very well. You may not realize it, but your father and I are the same age. We actually attended school together for much of our lives."

"Then how come I hadn't heard of you until just a few days ago?"

"That's part of the story. I don't think your father thinks that I uphold the Letterford name in proper fashion."

"It's very important to him," noted Colophon.

"As well it should be," replied Julian. "He has the responsibility of running the entire business. I don't mean to diminish what he does or the value he attaches to our family name. I just couldn't bring myself to continue in the family business."

"But why?"

"It was my senior year in college. There I was, ready to graduate. After graduation I was supposed to go to work for the family business, just like every other Letterford. No one ever asked what I was going to do after college—they already knew. I would have started out in a low-paying job in marketing or promotion, and I would eventually work my way up to a position as a senior editor."

Julian paused.

"I simply realized that my whole life was mapped out for me."

"Is that so bad?" asked Colophon.

He looked at her. "It's *horrible*. Life shouldn't follow a script—particularly a script written by someone else."

"So," replied Colophon, "am I some sort of mindless robot for wanting to be part of the family business?"

"No, as long as that is your decision."

"It is."

"Then," said Julian, "pursue it with all the passion in the world."

Colophon sat back in her seat. The countryside rolled past her window.

"My brother doesn't want to follow the script. He says he has no interest in the family business."

"Good for him! Let him set his own course."

"But he's such a jerk. You just don't understand. He always has to make some comment about the way I dress, my glasses, my name—everything."

"Have you ever considered," asked Julian, "whether the script he has been handed is one that he truly wants? You may want to be part of the family business, but does he?"

"Are you saying he's a jerk because he feels like he's being forced into the family business?"

"Perhaps. Or he might just be a jerk. Just something to think about."

"Trust me—he's a jerk."

"He might be," said Julian. "But he should have the right to decide which path his life will take, don't you agree?"

Colophon didn't answer.

CHAPTER TWENTY
Oh Villainy!

Palace Hotel, room 723
Wednesday, December 17
9:00 a.m.

Mull Letterford stood in front of the mirror and adjusted his tie, for the fifth or sixth time.

"What do you think? Do I go with the red tie or the blue tie? Red is supposed to be a power color. Blue seems calming. What about something completely different?"

"Dad, you look great—very professional," replied Case. "Don't worry, everything will be fine."

Mull Letterford took a deep breath and exhaled. "OK, you're right. The tie is fine. The suit is fine. And the shoes look like a million dollars. I think I'm ready."

Mull had been particularly impressed by the promptness with which his shoes had been cleaned the previous evening and by the quality of the shoe shine. The shoes looked practically brand new. He had rewarded the valet with a twenty-dollar tip, although, for some strange reason, the valet seemed reluctant, almost embarrassed, to accept it.

"Grab your bag, and let's hit the road," Mull said to Case as he headed for the door. "I feel good about this day."

Case grabbed his backpack. "I'm right behind you."

While his father was in the shower, Case had located the address for the restaurant where his father's meeting with O'Dally would take place. After he was dropped off at the museum, his plan was to wait about an hour and then make his way over to the restaurant. Not surprisingly, the Find Coffee app on his iPhone showed that there was a Starbucks just across the street from the restaurant. He could keep an eye out for anything suspicious from there.

Mull and Case walked down the hallway to the elevators. As they waited for the elevator to arrive, Mull asked his son whether he need a few extra dollars for lunch and whether his cell phone was fully charged in case there was an emergency.

"I'm fine, Dad, really," replied Case, "but I can always use a few extra bucks."

Mull chuckled and handed his son a twenty-dollar bill just as the elevator arrived. They stepped into the elevator, and Case pushed the button to take them to the lobby.

As they started to descend, Case noticed that a foul odor had started to creep into and fill the elevator.

Case looked over at his father. "Dad, do you . . ."

"Yes," Mull replied. "What is that smell?"

It grew worse as the elevator continued down to the lobby. It consumed every square inch of the elevator. Case found it difficult to breathe. He looked over and noticed that his father was red-faced from holding his breath.

Mercifully, the elevator finally reached the ground floor. As the doors opened, the pungent smell that had collected in the elevator burst forth into the small elevator lobby. There were four guests and a bellboy waiting for elevators. They instantly reacted to the smell.

"I'm going to throw up!" one man exclaimed.

The other man standing in the lobby did just that.

A lady screamed in horror.

The bellboy abandoned his luggage cart and ran off.

Another lady fainted.

In short, pandemonium ensued among the small group unfortunate enough to be in the elevator lobby at that time. Case and Mull quickly stepped out into the main lobby, the smell trailing behind them.

"Case, is that you?" Mull asked.

Case smelled himself. Some of the odor lingered on him, but he clearly wasn't the source of the smell. He looked at his father, and his heart sank.

"Dad, I think it's—"

"Me," Mull Letterford said. "It's me."

Case sniffed his father, which made for an exceedingly odd image in the middle of the grand hotel's lobby. Guests—at least those far enough away—stared and pointed. Those unfortunate souls who were closer, however, reacted by gagging and holding their noses.

"It's your feet," said Case, who could barely breathe due to the stench. It was overpowering. "Take off your shoes."

Mull Letterford quickly removed his shoes.

131

Case smelled them. Had he already eaten breakfast, he would have lost it at that point. Dry heaves were his substitute.

By this point a number of hotel staff had come within a general circumference of Mull Letterford but would venture no closer than fifteen feet or so.

"Sir," said someone who appeared to be a manager, "you must leave the lobby immediately! The smell—it is overpowering."

"Case," said Mull, "grab the shoes, and let's head out to the courtyard."

They headed up the stairs and out into the courtyard outside the hotel's main entrance. However, even with his shoes removed, each footstep left a reminder of the pungent, putrid, rancid smell that emanated from Mull's feet. Once out in the courtyard, Mull quickly removed his socks, even though the temperature hovered just above freezing.

"Can you still smell it?" asked Mull.

Case bent over and took a big whiff of his father's foot. He almost gagged.

"No need to answer," said Mull. "Let's head back to the room and try to wash this off."

They were met at the door by the manager of the hotel. "I'm sorry," he said, "but I cannot allow you back in the lobby."

Case could see employees of the hotel vigorously mopping the floor behind the manager.

"But I have to get back to my room," Mull pleaded.

"Again, I'm sorry, but that . . . smell . . . it won't come off the floor. I cannot allow you back in the hotel under these circumstances."

Mull turned to Case and handed him the key. "Go back to the room and get me an extra pair of socks and my tennis shoes. I have a bottle of cologne in my overnight bag. Bring it with you as well. I'll wait out here."

Case headed back into the hotel. The whole lobby reeked. He ran into the elevator lobby, where members of the hotel staff were attempting to calm several outraged guests. Seconds later an elevator appeared. Fortunately, it was not the same elevator that they had taken down to the lobby. The ride up seemed to take forever. Finally the doors cracked open, and Case rushed down the hall to their room. He quickly located an extra pair of socks, his father's tennis shoes, and the bottle of cologne.

Back downstairs, Case found his father sitting on the far side of the courtyard, his feet in a bucket of hot, soapy water.

"The hotel was kind enough to bring this out to me," Mull said as he pointed to the bucket and a stack of towels lying next to it. "I think it may be working," he said optimistically. "Grab one of the towels, and let's check."

Case handed a towel to his father, who then proceeded to dry off each foot.

"OK," Case said, "let's see if we can still smell it."

Case closed his eyes and took a deep sniff. For the briefest of seconds—very brief indeed—Case had the illusion that it had worked. That thought came to a devastating end as the pungent odor of his father's feet once again assaulted his olfactory sense.

There was no need to state the obvious. The smell remained—as strong or stronger than before.

"Let's try the cologne," suggested Mull. "Maybe we can't kill the smell, but we can sure try to cover it up—at least long enough to get through my meeting."

Case took the bottle of cologne—a lime scent—and carefully placed a couple of drops on each foot.

"This is not the time for half measures," Mull said. "Dump the whole thing."

Case unscrewed the top of the green bottle and proceeded to pour half on one foot and half on the other. Mull then took a towel and used it to spread the cologne over each foot, between his toes, and up each ankle.

"Quick," Mull said, "hand me the clean socks before this stuff dries completely."

Case handed his father the pair of socks he had retrieved.

"Now the tennis shoes," Mull said.

Case handed his father the tennis shoes.

Mull stood up. "OK," he said, "how is it now?"

What Case smelled and saw was disaster. The pungent smell remained; now, however, it was highlighted by a lime scent that reeked of rotten fruit. His father's appearance was equally disarming. From the belt line up, Mull looked every bit the businessman that he was. From the belt line down, it was a different story. The steam from the bucket had wrinkled Mull's pants, which, to be fair, were already soaked from sitting on a wet bench in the courtyard. He wore a pair of dingy white running shoes and white socks.

And he stank.

He stank bad.

Mull Letterford did not wait for an answer—the look on his son's face was clear enough. It was, however, now nine-thirty a.m., and he could no longer sit around in the hotel's courtyard. He needed to head in the direction of his meeting. He would try to figure something out once he was near the restaurant.

"C'mon, let's grab a cab," Mull said to his son as he stepped out into Madison Avenue. He threw up his right arm, and almost immediately, a bright yellow taxicab pulled up to the curb. Mull and Case climbed into the back.

"Where ya heading?" asked the cab driver.

"Natural History Museum," replied Mull.

The cab pulled away from the curb—and then pulled right back over.

"Get out of the cab," the driver said.

"Why?" asked Mull, although he knew exactly why.

"You smell," the driver replied. "You smell bad."

"But I have to get to the museum," replied Mull.

"Good for you," replied the driver, "but you're not doing it in my cab. Now get out."

Mull and Case exited the cab. After two more failed attempts at securing a cab, they had barely made it one block. They stood on the sidewalk.

"We're going to have to walk," Mull said.

"But Dad, the museum is more than thirty blocks away. Can't we take the subway?"

"Not unless you want to start a riot. I don't think we have much choice. We need to get started."

Mull Letterford looked down at his shoes and grimaced. "Good thing I have my walking shoes on."

CHAPTER TWENTY-ONE
A Monument Upon Thy Bones

IVDICIO PYLIVM GENIO SOCRATEM ARTE MARONEM
TERRA TEGIT, POPVLVS MÆRET, OLYMPVS HABE

STAY PASSENGER, WHY GOEST THOV BY SO FAST,
READ IF THOU CANST, WHOM ENVIOUS DEATH HATH PLAST
WITH IN THIS MONUMENT SHAKESPEARE: WITH WHOME,
QUICK NATURE DIDE WHOSE NAME DOTH DECK Y TOMBE,
FAR MORE THEN COST: SIEH ALL Y HE, HATH WRITT,
LEAVES LIVING ART, BVT PAGE, TO SERVE HIS WITT.

Stratford-upon-Avon, England
Wednesday, December 17

Colophon and Julian arrived in Stratford-upon-Avon in the late afternoon. The day was cold, overcast, gray, and wet—the usual conditions for much of

England. As they crossed the Avon, Colophon could make out the tall spire of the church rising along the banks of the river. Dusk was setting in quickly, so the duo wasted no time in parking the car and heading to Holy Trinity Church, the location of Shakespeare's monument. Before leaving the car, Julian retrieved a well-worn leather backpack from the trunk and threw it over his shoulder.

"That thing is huge," said Colophon. "What do you carry in it?"

"Oh, the usual," replied Julian. "A couple of bottles of water, my journal, my backup journal, flashlights, a map, my Swiss army knife, chewing gum, breath mints, a GPS locator, tracing paper, a camera, trail mix—the kind with cranberries—tissues, my Fiji Islands good luck charm, my cell phone, an extra cell phone, and—"

Colophon rolled her eyes. "Forget I asked—let's just get to the church."

The entrance to the church was located at the end of a long stone pathway lined with large weathered gravestones. Everything seemed to take on a gray, flat tone.

Colophon grabbed Julian's hand as they walked along the path. "The tombstones are kinda spooky, don't you think?"

"Of comfort no man speak," replied Julian. "Let's talk of graves, of worms, and epitaphs."

"Gross. Shakespeare?" asked Colophon.

"Yes, from *King Richard II*."

"Are you going to keep quoting Shakespeare?"

"Probably," replied Julian.

A small group of tourists mingled outside the church as they approached the entrance. The large wooden door creaked slightly as Julian pushed it open and they stepped inside. The light was dim, and it took a couple of minutes for Colophon's eyes to adjust.

"Do we just wander around until we find the monument?" Colophon whispered.

"Apparently there is an admission price," said Julian. He pointed to a sign that requested a donation of £1.50 for adults and 50 pence for students. "Maybe they'll have a guidebook. Wait here while I go pay."

Julian walked over to a small stand and returned shortly thereafter with a brochure.

"Well," said Julian, "according to this guidebook, the monument is located in the chancel."

"What's the chancel?" asked Colophon.

"Follow me," replied Julian as they walked to the center of the church. "The church is shaped like a cross. Many old churches and cathedrals were constructed in that basic shape. This long central hall is where the congregation sits. It's the longest part of the cross. It's called the nave. The short parts of the cross, which extend off to either side of the nave, are the transepts. Now, Shakespeare's monument is located in the chancel, which is located at the top of the cross, separated from the nave by the crossing of the transept."

Colophon and Julian walked slowly up the center of the nave toward the crossing of the transept. Now that her eyes had adjusted to the dim light, Colophon realized that there were a number of other visitors in the church.

"This place seems really popular," she said.

"I should say so. Just think about it. In this very building are buried the remains of the greatest playwright who ever lived. This is where he was baptized, this is where he worshiped as a young boy, and this is where he was buried. Did you know that they still have the record of his baptism from 1564?"

"Wow," said Colophon.

Julian stopped and looked down at Colophon. "It's one thing to read about history. This *is* history. Construction of this church started almost eight hundred years ago. Eight hundred years! And—what's even more remarkable—this building was built on the remains of an old Saxon church. You are literally walking through history. Look at this stone floor. Thousands upon thousands of people have walked through this church and across this stone floor. Kings, queens, presidents, and William Shakespeare have walked these stones. Shakespeare was not simply some abstract, fictional character from history. He was a real man. And this is where he lived, breathed, worshiped, and died. This was already an old church when he was alive."

Julian looked around.

"So much in this world does not seem real," he continued. "We think we are so connected nowadays— cell phones, Internet, and constant access to everything and everybody. But we're not really connected. We've forgotten what's real. We've forgotten how to interact with the world around us. Not just to see something on a screen but to feel it, to smell it, to taste it. That's reality."

Julian bent down to the floor and motioned for Colophon to do the same. "Touch the floor."

She put her hand on the cold stone floor. It was smooth and cool to the touch.

"This floor has been here for almost eight hundred years. Shakespeare walked on it. At some point,

Shakespeare may have stood in this very spot and looked at the same thing you are looking at."

Colophon closed her eyes. The whispers of the other people and the other sounds melted into the background. She could feel the coolness of the stone floor. She could smell the faint odor of the thousands upon thousands of candles burned over the centuries in the church. She felt herself transported back hundreds of years. Julian was right. History was alive in a place like this. Shakespeare was not simply a character in some story. Here, he felt real.

"Can I help you?"

The voice startled Colophon, and she fell back onto the floor. She looked up to see a white-haired man in a black clerical robe staring down at her.

"Terribly sorry, young miss—I didn't mean to startle you. I just wanted to make sure you were OK. I'm Reverend Mackey, the vicar here at Holy Trinity."

"Not a problem at all," interjected Julian. "We were having a bit of a history lesson. You know—here is where Shakespeare walked, worshiped, and all that."

"I completely understand. To tell the truth, I guess I take it for granted, having worked here for so long. However, I must confess that I once touched an Egyptian sarcophagus at the British Museum just to see what it felt like. Received quite a scolding from the guard. But it was worth it."

Colophon pulled herself up and stood in front of the reverend.

"Actually, maybe you can help us. We're looking for the Shakespeare monument," Colophon said.

"That's odd," replied Reverend Mackey.

"Why?"

"Well, it's just that most people ask to see his grave, not the monument."

"I'm confused," she said. "Aren't they the same thing?"

"No," said Reverend Mackey. "The monument was actually erected several years after his death."

"Which one has a poem on it?" asked Julian.

Reverend Mackey smiled. "Again, I don't mean to cause more confusion than necessary, but both of them have poems. Now, the fact that you have actually inquired about one of the poems is intriguing in and of itself. I certainly can't let a budding scholar flounder on her own. I guess we'd better look at both of the poems and see exactly which one you are looking for. Why don't we start with the grave? But we need to hurry. Closing time is almost upon us."

He led them over to the church chancel. Colophon was speechless. The chancel was stunning. The high walls were lined with tall stained-glass windows that shimmered with color from the last flickers of daylight. Candles burned throughout the room, lending a golden glow to the otherwise pale limestone walls. A short brass rail, however, prevented access to the heart of the room.

Reverend Mackey pointed to a small sign on the floor just beyond the low rail. It read THE GRAVE OF THE POET WILLIAM SHAKESPEARE — 1564–1616.

"He's buried in the floor of the church?" asked Colophon.

"Yes, around twenty feet or so below your feet," replied the Reverend. "And his wife Anne is buried there to the left, and his son-in-law to the right. That was quite a common practice back in the day. There are bodies buried all throughout this building. But do you know why Shakespeare was buried here in the chancel?"

"Because he was so famous?" replied Colophon.

"Well, he may have been famous, but that's not why he's buried here."

"Then why?"

"The Bard is buried here because he actually purchased part of the taxing privileges for the church. You see, in his day Shakespeare was known for being a businessman as much as a playwright, although many of his fans are loath to admit it. They think it tarnishes his image—not very romantic, you see. But the truth is that playwrights were considered an unsavory lot back in his time. And to make matters worse, he was also an actor. Quite a disreputable group in the sixteenth century."

"An actor?" replied Colophon. "I didn't know that."

"Most people don't," said Reverend Mackey. "But you must forgive—I do tend to ramble." He pointed to a plaque on the grave. "Is that, perhaps, the poem you are looking for?"

The poem read:

> *Good frend for Jesus sake forbeare*
> *To digg the dust encloased heare.*
> *Blese be ye man yt spares thes stones,*
> *And curst be he yt moves my bones.*

"That's the wrong poem," said Colophon. She looked at Reverend Mackey. "Is that a curse?"

"Of sorts, I suppose," he replied. "Shakespeare was very concerned that someone would dig up his remains. That's one of the reasons he is buried so deep. He reportedly wrote the poem himself as a warning to would-be grave robbers."

"That's creepy."

"Creepy indeed, but it has apparently worked. His bones have remained undisturbed for close to four hundred years. Now, let's see if we can find the poem you're looking for. Perhaps it's the poem on the Shakespeare Monument."

Reverend Mackey turned to his left and pointed to the wall of the chancel. "And there, dear girl, is the Shakespeare Monument."

High in a recess in the wall was a full-size painted sculpture of William Shakespeare—at least from the waist up. He was dressed in red and black with a starched white collar, a quill in his right hand and a piece of paper in his left. Beneath the sculpture was an inscribed plate that read:

IVDICIO PYLIUM, GENIO SOCRATEM,
   ARTE MARONEM,
TERRA TEGIT, POPULUS MAERET,
   OLYMPUS HABET

STAY PASSENGER, WHY GOEST THOV
BY SO FAST?

READ IF THOV CANST, WHOM EN-
VIOVS DEATH HATH PLAST
WITH IN THIS MONVMENT SHAK-
SPEARE: WITH WHOME,
QVICK NATVRE DIDE: WHOSE NAME,
DOTH DECK YS TOMBE,
FAR MORE, THEN COST: SIEH ALL,
YT HE HATH WRITT,
LEAVES LIVING ART, BVT PAGE, TO
SERVE HIS WITT.

Colophon looked at the reverend. "Is that the poem?" she asked. She was an excellent reader—the best in her class—but most of the inscription didn't seem to make sense.

He gave a short laugh. "Not exactly modern English, is it?" he said. "The second part, as you can probably tell, is a poem. In modern English, it would read:

"Stay, passenger, why goest thou by so fast?
Read, if thou canst, whom envious Death hath placed
Within this monument: Shakespeare, with whom
Quick nature died, whose name doth deck this tomb
Far more than cost, since all that he hath writ
Leaves living art, but page, to serve his wit."

147

Colophon listened closely and absorbed every word. The poem on the monument seemed so similar to the poem from Miles Letterford's portrait. Could this be the next clue?

"What about the first part?" she asked. "That's Latin, right?"

"Yes," interjected Julian, "and with the good reverend's permission, may I take a stab at it?"

"Stab away," replied Reverend Mackey.

Julian adjusted his glasses and read: "'A Pylos in judgment, a Socrates in genius, a Maro in art. The earth buries him, the people mourn him, Olympus possesses him.'"

"Very nice," said Reverend Mackey.

"Well, this is certainly the poem we've been looking for," said Colophon. She wondered whether Miles Letterford would use another poem as a clue. Perhaps there was something else. "Is there anything about the monument that is—well—unusual or strange?"

"That's the first time anyone has asked me that particular question."

"So, nothing strange?"

"Actually," replied Reverend Mackey, "there are a few items that some people might consider odd. For example, did you notice the skull on top of the monument?"

"A skull?" She had not noticed it.

"Yes, a skull," replied the reverend. He moved Colophon and Julian back away from the monument and then pointed. There, sitting on the very top of the monument, was a human skull.

"Why did they carve a skull into the monument?" Colophon asked.

"Oh, that skull is not carved," replied Reverend Mackey. "It's a real skull."

"A real skull!" she exclaimed. "Whose skull is it?" Maybe it was the next clue.

Reverend Mackey shrugged. "No one is really sure, and no one knows exactly what it means."

Colophon was disappointed. "Is there anything else odd about the monument?"

"Well," he replied, "as you can see, the final line of the poem references a single page written by Shakespeare, not his entire body of work. That has always struck me as strange, considering the volumes and volumes he produced. Why erect a monument to a single page? And what page?"

"That does seem odd," said Colophon.

"And," Reverend Mackey continued, "do you see that piece of paper in Shakespeare's hand?"

Colophon nodded. "Is that the page mentioned in the poem?"

"That would seem to make sense, but there's nothing written on it. Not a single word."

"Perhaps it was painted on and has worn away with time," suggested Julian.

"Others have entertained that same thought, but I'm afraid not," replied the reverend. "As far as we've been able to determine, it has always been blank. And no one is quite sure why. In the end, it is a mystery—and we must accept it as such."

"Is there anything else?" asked Julian.

"Well, the monument itself has been through quite an ordeal since it was placed here in the early seventeenth century. The quill has been stolen several times and replaced. In the nineteen seventies, thieves actually removed the sculpture from the wall in an effort to locate manuscripts that they believed were hidden inside the monument. Of course, they didn't find anything. And then there's one last bit of trivia that you might be interested in. See that door to the left?"

Julian and Colophon both looked at the large wooden door, below and to the left of the monument.

"Do you know where it leads?" asked Reverend Mackey.

"Outside?" asked Colophon.

"It leads nowhere," replied the reverend.

"Nowhere?"

"Nowhere," he repeated. "It used to lead into a small storage building that held a set of stairs that went down to a crypt below this very room. When the storage building was torn down, the door was bricked up from the outside."

"What about the crypt?" asked Colophon.

"Still down there, I suppose, but no one is really sure. If we started digging under the foundations of a church this old, who knows what would happen? I don't think anyone wants to be responsible for the floor collapsing—or worse."

Reverend Mackey looked down at his watch.

"I do apologize for monopolizing your time," he said. "I've bored you good folks long enough, and I must tend to my duties before the church closes. I do hope you enjoy your visit to our fair church."

"It has been our pleasure meeting you," said Julian.

"Yes," chimed in Colophon, "and thank you for all your help and information."

"Remember," said Reverend Mackey, "we will be closing in ten minutes. I hate to rush you, but—as they say—rules are rules."

And with a slight bow in Colophon's direction, he departed. Colophon waited until he was back in the nave before she turned to Julian and said, "I don't get the first part of the inscription. I heard you mention Socrates, but what about King Nestor and Virgil?"

"Ah yes," replied Julian, "that does appear a bit confusing, although it really is not. You see, Nestor was the king of Pylos."

"What about Maro?"

"What is your last name?" asked Julian.

"You know very well what my last name is."

"Of course I do," replied Julian, "just as you now know Virgil's last name."

"Maro," answered Colophon with a grin.

Chapter Twenty-Two
Let Slip the Dogs of War

Central Park, heading east
New York City
Wednesday, December 17

Janice Waterstone struggled to maintain control over the five dogs that she was attempting to walk through Central Park.

Twenty-two years old. An art degree from NYU. Fluent in French.

Walking dogs for rich people.

Perfect. Just perfect.

She watched as a large golden retriever named Max excused himself on the grass for what seemed like the tenth time that morning.

What do they feed him?

She pulled a plastic bag out of her pocket and prepared to scoop up the remains.

It can't get any worse than this.

And yet it did get worse.

Janice didn't see Mull Letterford pass by her, but she sure smelled him.

So did the dogs.

All at once, the five dogs tethered to Janice lurched in Mull's direction. Janice, who was bending over to clean up after Max, fell backwards and lost her grip on the leashes.

All five dogs broke loose at once.

Central Park, heading west
New York City
Wednesday, December 17
11:00 a.m.

With all the background noise in New York City, the sound of the barking dogs did not instantly register with Case. However, as the barking grew louder (and closer), he turned to discover that they were being approached by a pack of dogs led by a large golden retriever.

"Dad!" cried Case. "Watch out!"

But it was too late. The dogs—all of them—hit Mull Letterford at full tilt. Mull fell backwards and tumbled down a muddy embankment. He rolled over and over until he landed face first in a shallow pool of dirty rainwater at the bottom of the hill.

Case scrambled down the embankment and pulled his father to his knees. He glanced back up. At the top of the embankment, more dogs were beginning to descend.

"Run!" Case yelled.

And so he and Mull did.

They headed north along a path through the park. Case glanced back over his shoulder. The dogs were gaining ground rapidly, empty leashes flailing from their necks. The pack seemed to be growing—as was the group of annoyed dog owners in fast pursuit of their charges. Case accelerated to catch up to his dad.

The barking grew closer with every step. Case realized that it was only a matter of time before the dogs caught up with them. They needed to do something—and do it fast. Ahead and to his left, Case spied what appeared to be a large playground. "This way!" he yelled as he took a sharp left turn through a covered walkway and into the playground.

With the sudden change in direction, a dog in the lead stepped on the loose leash of another. The leash pulled tight, and several dogs tripped over it and became entangled. The momentum of the dogs was too great for them to stop. Case could hear yelps and yips as the dogs piled one on top of another behind him. Seizing the opportunity, he and his father sprinted across the playground, past several confused children and their parents, and toward a large rock outcropping that marked the playground's far boundary. If they could make it up the rock and into the woods before the dogs regrouped, they might have a chance.

No such luck.

The dogs quickly untangled and, after a brief moment of confusion, resumed their pursuit. Case and his father scrambled up the rock. The barking grew louder behind them.

"Hurry!" Case yelled. "They're coming!"

He reached the top of the rock and turned to look at his father. Mull Letterford—weighed down by his heavy wet clothes—was struggling to make it to the top. The dogs had now reached the base of the rock and were starting to clamber and claw their way toward Mull.

There was no way they were going to make it to the restaurant in time.

CHAPTER TWENTY-THREE
Unquiet Meals Make Ill Digestions

Deorio's Italian Restaurant
New York City
Wednesday, December 17
11:15 a.m.

"Welcome back, Mr. O'Dally," the maître d' said as he
opened the door to the restaurant. "We are so hon-

ored that you are joining us for lunch today. It has been a while since you last dined with us."

Patrick O'Dally looked like an uptight high school math teacher from the 1950s. He was fifty-nine years old but seemed at least a generation older. His black hair was combed back tightly against his head and held in place by some sort of cream. He wore a red bow tie, a white shirt, a black jacket, crisply ironed gray pants, and a pair of highly polished shoes.

O'Dally peered over the top of his glasses at the maître d'. "I assume you have corrected the problem?"

The "problem" that had plagued O'Dally on his last visit to the restaurant was that his table was not ready at precisely the time he had requested. His reservation had been at 11:15 a.m. His table had been ready at 11:16 a.m. It was, in O'Dally's opinion, an outrage. That had been over a year ago. Under most circumstances, the restaurant owners would have lost no sleep over the loss of such a customer. O'Dally was, in many ways, a complete distraction every time he entered the restaurant. However, in addition to penning a number of best-selling novels, he also blogged daily — in excruciating detail — about his every meal. His blog was followed by millions of gourmands across the planet. Even the slightest hint that a restaurant had not met his exacting standards could result in a dramatic drop in business.

"You have my personal assurance that the problem has been corrected," replied the maître d'. "If you will follow me, your table is ready."

Actually, the table had been ready since the restaurant closed the night before. It was not simply that O'Dally demanded that everything in his life follow a specific timetable. No, everything had to be done in a specific manner. The linens on the table had been ironed the previous evening, with each corner folded over right to left in the postmodern fashion, not left to right. The table setting was carefully measured to ensure that each element was appropriately and proportionately spaced on the table—according, of course, to the basic requirements of service *à la russe*.

Normally only one place setting was set up, lest the removal of another place setting leave an unseemly indention in the linens. However, because O'Dally was going to be joined for lunch, two identical place settings were set up. O'Dally surveyed the table as the maître d' anxiously watched. "It is acceptable," O'Dally finally pronounced as he sat down. "My guest should arrive within the next fifteen minutes."

✣ ✣ ✣

"Dad!" Case yelled. "Climb!"

But Mull Letterford did not climb the rock. In fact, he sat down.

"Dad!" Case pleaded.

But Mull ignored him.

The dogs were now just a few yards away. All Case could do was stand there and watch.

And then, just as the dogs were about to reach him, Mull Letterford stood up and, with a quick motion, tossed something over their heads. The dogs stopped instantly, turned around, and headed back down the rock.

It took a second for Case to realize what had occurred.

And then it hit him—his father was now barefoot. The dogs were fighting over Mull Letterford's shoes and socks in the playground below.

"Let's go!" Mull yelled as he scrambled over the top of the rock and leaped into the woods. Case turned and ran after him. Within minutes they were out of the park and heading north along Central Park West. They slowed their pace to a quick walk as they caught their breath. Case looked at his father. He was bruised, scraped, disheveled, and shoeless. Case knew he was freezing.

"Do you think we lost them?" Mull asked.

"I don't know," Case replied. "You still smell like roadkill—and I don't think there were enough shoes and socks to satisfy that crowd."

He looked back to see if they were being followed. There was a jogger, a woman pushing a stroller, a group of teenagers, and an elderly couple walking hand in hand—but no dogs.

Relieved, Case turned to tell his father the good news.

And that's when he heard it.

It was faint, but Case knew exactly what it was—a dog's bark. Mull Letterford heard it too. In unison, they turned and looked back down the sidewalk. Half a block behind them—at the same spot where they had exited the park—a small dog scampered out onto the sidewalk. It stopped, put its nose in the air, and turned toward Case and his father. For a moment there was silence. Everything was still. The dog stared at them, and they at the dog. And then it started.

Suddenly dogs of every size, color, and breed

poured out of Central Park and headed directly toward them. Case and his father broke into a sprint. Behind them, the symphony of car horns, angry shouts, and barking dogs was deafening. Case and his father scrambled between cars to cross the avenue and headed down a side street.

The dogs followed.

They reached Columbus Avenue at the end of the block and turned north. They were less than a block from the restaurant, but the dogs remained in determined pursuit.

"There!" yelled Mull Letterford. "There's the restaurant!"

Mull burst into the front of the restaurant, while Case braced himself at the entrance for the onslaught of canines that was rapidly descending upon him.

Pat O'Dally pulled out his pocket watch and glanced down at it. It was 11:28 a.m. The restaurant was already packed with the usual crowd of locals and a handful of tourists.

But no Letterford.

O'Dally put his pocket watch away and surveyed the table. Over the course of the last few minutes, he had made numerous minor adjustments to the placement of the utensils and the fold of the napkins. Everything was perfect and in its place, except for the empty seat directly across from him.

O'Dally pulled out his pocket watch again.

It was now 11:29 a.m.

O'Dally started to put his watch away when he heard a loud voice from the front of the restaurant.

"Sir! You can't—"

This exclamation was followed by footsteps coming toward O'Dally's private room, the sounds of a tray falling and glass breaking, and several more gruff comments. The noise stopped, and after a brief moment of silence, the door to the private dining room opened. In the doorway stood a middle-aged man, his salt-and-pepper hair dripping with sweat and sticking out in all directions. He wore a muddy gray suit that looked as if it had been crumpled in a gym bag for a week. A red tie hung asunder from his neck. He was barefoot. And he stank. He stank really bad.

It was, O'Dally realized, Mull Letterford.

"I am . . . ," Mull panted, "here."

O'Dally—notwithstanding the initial shock of Letterford's entrance, his appearance, and his odor—glanced calmly down at his watch. It was now 11:31 a.m.

Letterford was late.

O'Dally started to admonish Letterford for his breach of etiquette when he was interrupted by the sounds of sirens blaring, dogs barking, and people yelling.

Was there a parade? O'Dally wondered. Perhaps a fire?

The noise grew louder.

"Can we speak about the contract?" Mull Letterford panted as he nervously looked back over his shoulder.

Again, O'Dally started to open his mouth. The noise, however, grew even louder—and closer.

And then things got worse.

A small terrier came running into the room and jumped onto the dining table. The dog glanced briefly in O'Dally's direction, turned, and started barking at Mull Letterford.

Letterford and O'Dally stared at each other and then at the dog on the table.

And that's when it happened.

A tsunami of dogs flooded the restaurant. There was a crash of glass and tables.

Pasta flew everywhere.

Sparkling water spilled from every table.

Waiters slipped.

Meatballs shot through the air.

Spaghetti sauce splattered across the walls.

And Parmesan cheese dusted everything in sight.

It was a culinary and literary disaster, the likes of which had not been seen since the unfortunate Hemingway-gorgonzola incident of '48.

O'Dally sat in his chair. Several large dogs surrounded Mull and barked intensely at his feet.

"I don't know what to say," Mull shouted above the barking.

O'Dally stood up, straightened his jacket, and turned to Mull. "There is," O'Dally said bluntly, "nothing to say. You were late by fifteen seconds."

And with that, he stepped over several dogs and between two fallen waiters and exited the restaurant.

Chapter Twenty-Four
With Hidden Help and Vantage

Holy Trinity Church
Stratford-upon-Avon
Wednesday, December 17

"OK," said Colophon, "so we're in the right place. What next? The poem? It seems like it could be full of clues. And look around this room — carvings, graves, and stained glass. They could all be clues. Where do we even begin?"

Julian and Colophon turned and stared at the Shakespeare monument.

"It has to be the monument," said Julian. "Perhaps something is hidden in the statue?" Julian paused. "It could be anything. My guess is that the clue is staring right at us. The reason I couldn't find the clue in the portrait of Miles Letterford was because I tried too hard — I was looking for hidden clues and codes. But the real clue was right in front of me the whole time. It was a brilliant move on the part of Miles Letterford. I suspect that the same approach will apply here. The next clue is probably right in front of us."

"OK," replied Colophon, "let's look at what we have. The inscription appears to refer to a single page."

"Correct," agreed Julian.

"And," she continued, "the sculpture shows Shakespeare holding a single piece of paper."

"Correct."

"And yet," she said, "the paper is blank."

They stared at the sculpture.

"I want to see it," Colophon said.

Julian looked around. No one was in the immediate vicinity of the monument. The church would be closing in mere minutes.

"Go quick, before anyone comes."

She scooted over the brass rail that separated viewers from the monument and approached it. Next to the monument was a large marble ossuary. She climbed quickly on top of it and examined the paper held under the statue's left hand.

She looked over at Julian and whispered: "Nothing." Then she retreated back over the rail. "So again, what next?" she asked Julian. "We're running out of time."

They continued to stare at the monument. Just then the bells of the church started to ring.

"Closing time," said Julian.

They could hear the church volunteers politely asking other visitors to exit. In only a matter of moments, they would reach the chancel.

"But we haven't figured it out yet!" Colophon protested.

"No, we haven't," replied Julian. "But unless your plans involve hiding in this church, I suggest we depart."

She started to object, but stopped and simply nodded.

✦ ✦ ✦

Case paced outside the restaurant waiting for his father. Policemen, firefighters, employees of the restaurant, and irate dog owners worked diligently outside the restaurant and around the block to bring some order to the chaos. To his credit, Case had made a noble, and completely unsuccessful, effort to keep the dogs from entering the restaurant. Now he didn't have the heart to look inside. The front door opened, and Mull Letterford walked out.

"Dad?"

Mull walked over to his son.

"Dad," asked Case, "are you OK?"

Mull looked down at his watch and wiped a meatball from his forearm. He was covered in red sauce. Spaghetti hung from his shoulder. A Boykin spaniel sniffed persistently at his feet. He appeared stunned.

"I'm fine," he finally answered in a quiet, resigned voice. "We need to get you over to the museum so that you can work on your report. I'm sorry—I should have had you at the museum this morning."

Case stared at his father. Obviously, he did not get the contract. That meant he was one step closer to losing the family business. And yet, Case realized, despite all that had occurred this morning, his father was still concerned about him.

"The report can wait," Case said. "Let's get you back to the hotel—it's been a long morning."

Mull Letterford looked down at his son and nodded. "It has been a very long morning."

Stratford-upon-Avon
Wednesday, December 17

Colophon and Julian stepped out of the church and started down the long path through the graveyard. Although it was early evening, a full moon illuminated the path and the graveyard. It had turned very cold.

"Are you OK?" asked Julian.

Colophon stopped and looked down at her feet. "I—I just thought the clue would jump out at us. I was so sure."

He bent down and looked at her. "I know. I was certain we'd find something. Some hint of a new clue. I guess I forgot how hard this journey really can be."

Colophon stared straight ahead over his shoulder into the graveyard beyond. Her face betrayed no emotion.

"Listen," he continued. "Perhaps your mother will let us come back here in a day or so. We can spend some more time in the chancel. Maybe something new will turn up."

Colophon continued to stare straight ahead.

"Are you all right?" asked Julian.

She looked at him. A slight grin crossed her face.

"I've found the next clue."

Before he could comprehend exactly what Colophon had said, she had sprinted past him into the graveyard.

"Wait!" Julian yelled. But she was already several yards into the graveyard and moving quickly between the headstones. He gathered his backpack and headed after her. He found her less than a hundred feet from the path, standing in front of a mausoleum.

"Colophon, you can't run off like that. Your mother would absolutely—"

Colophon pointed to the family name on the mausoleum, carved into the marble exterior.

WITT.

He stared at the name.

"This has to be it," she said. "The name is the same as the last line of the poem on the monument: *'Leaves living art, but page, to serve his WITT.'*"

"It can't be that simple," he stammered.

"Look at the date on the mausoleum," she said.

Julian looked at the bronze door. It read simply 1623 — the same year the Shakespeare Monument had been erected.

"Well, I'll be."

"We have to get inside," said Colophon.

Julian stared at the door to the mausoleum.

"Well?" she asked.

Julian continued to stare at the door. Finally he looked at her and said: "I guess we'd better call your mom and tell her we're going to be late."

The Limpton Club
Boston, Massachusetts
December 17, noon

Treemont sat in a deep leather chair and peered out the window at the city of Boston. His gaze was unfocused. An unread newspaper sat on his lap. The reading room in the club was usually quiet at this time of day. The lunch crowd had all headed to the dining room, leaving Treemont alone, as he preferred.

His cell phone buzzed in his coat pocket. Although cell phones were forbidden in the club, none of the staff had the courage to enforce this rule when it came to Treemont.

He looked at the number on his phone. "Yes?" he said.

"It's done," James replied.

"How was it?"

"Spectacular. Want to see the video?"

"Video?" replied Treemont. "You videoed it?"

"Of course."

"Send it to the secure e-mail," Treemont responded before ending the call without another word.

A moment later Treemont's cell phone buzzed yet again. This time it was to notify him that he had received an e-mail. He took a look around the reading room to confirm that he was alone before opening the attachment. The video played across the phone's small screen.

"Spectacular indeed," Treemont said to himself. He returned his gaze to the city beyond and contemplated the days to come.

Be forewarned those who seek the page
Travel swift,
lest time preserve ye for all age.

Stratford-upon-Avon

Wednesday, December 17

It took less than two minutes for Julian to pick the lock to the mausoleum door.

"I'm impressed," said Colophon.

"Well," he replied, "I have picked up a useful skill

or two in my travels. Just don't mention this particular skill to your mother, OK?"

"Our secret," she assured him.

He looked around the graveyard and church grounds. There was no one in sight. He gave a tug on the door, which reluctantly swung open a foot or so. He retrieved a flashlight from his backpack.

"Wait here for a second," he said as he stepped into the dark interior. A moment later he stuck his head out the door: "Quick, step inside. It looks safe."

Colophon stepped into the mausoleum, as Julian pulled the door shut behind her. The room was cold. She could smell the dust and age of the stone crypt. He illuminated the room with his flashlight.

"More dead people," Colophon said.

"Yes," replied Julian. "More dead people."

The left and right walls of the mausoleum appeared to be divided into three tiers. A name and date of birth and death were engraved on each tier.

"Here, take this." Julian handed Colophon a flashlight from his backpack. "Look around and see if you see any clues."

Julian headed to the right side wall, and Colophon to the left.

Colophon read from top to bottom:

Hon. Adalmund Witt 1675–1723

Eadric Lyndon Witt 1700–1763

Deakin Newey Witt 1729–1801

There was no other ornamentation on the wall. No other writing.

"Nothing," Colophon announced. "I don't see anything here that looks like a clue."

Julian walked over to her. "Same on the other side," he said. "Just names and dates. Nothing else. Two down, one to go."

They swung their flashlights toward the back wall of the mausoleum. What they saw stopped them in their tracks.

There was only one inscription on the back wall, and it read:

Arthur Witt 1554–1623

May his memory live in our hearts forever.

Above the inscription was an oval brass plate with a large W engraved in the middle of it.

"Arthur Witt! Art Witt!" said Julian. "Incredible! Just like the poem from the monument: 'Leaves living *Art* to serve his *Witt*'! And look at the date of his death—1623—the same as Shakespeare's monument!"

"This *cannot* be a coincidence!" exclaimed Colophon. "This has to be the next clue."

"Oh, of that I am certain," responded Julian. "But I return to our favorite question—what next?"

They stood and stared at the wall in which Arthur Witt was apparently entombed.

Was there even a person by that name? Colophon wondered.

With their flashlights, they scanned the entire wall, looking for some clue or hint as to where Mr. Witt intended to take them next.

Nothing.

With the exception of the inscription and the brass plate, the wall was blank. Again, no mysterious ornamentation, carvings, or engravings. No buttons to push or Scooby-Doo-esque candlesticks to pull. Nothing. Just a gray, dusty, cobweb-covered wall.

And yet, thought Colophon, *something seems strangely familiar. But what?*

"We seem to spend a lot of time staring at walls," she said.

Julian chuckled. "Welcome to my world."

He looked down at his watch. "We don't have much

time. I promised your mother we'd be on the road by seven, and it's almost six-thirty-five right now."

"I know," replied Colophon. "But we are so—"she paused. *Could it be?*

"What?" asked Julian. "Do you see something?"

She cocked her head to the side, her flashlight illuminating the back wall. Julian looked from her to the wall and back.

"I have seen that W before," she said.

He turned his flashlight onto the brass plate.

"Where?" asked Julian. "In the church?"

"No," she replied. "In my father's office."

"What?" he asked. "You have seen that W in your father's office?"

"Not just the W," she replied. "The entire brass plate. My father has an exact copy."

He was stunned. "But how? Where?"

"And, for the record," she said, "it's not a W."

He turned the flashlight back to the brass plate. "What are you talking about? Of course it's a W."

Colophon walked over to the wall next to the brass plate. "No, it's not a W. I knew there was something very familiar about the W—the entire brass plate. I just wasn't sure why."

"I simply don't see where you are going with this."

"It's the key!" replied Colophon.

"The key to what?"

"No, not a key to something. It is the same symbol that's on the key—the Letterford key that my father keeps in his office."

"I don't understand."

Julian paused, then slowly cocked his head to the left. As he did so, the W transformed into a sigma —Σ—exactly the same as on the Letterford key. Even the brass plate—in an oval shape—matched the key.

"Remarkable," Julian muttered under his breath. "OK," he said. "Same question as before—"

"What next?" answered Colophon. She walked over to the wall, ran her hand across the brass plate, and then turned to face her cousin.

"I think," she said, "we need to straighten it out and see what happens."

"Just turn it?" he asked.

"Just turn it," she responded.

Julian walked over to the wall. Peering over his glasses, he closely examined the brass plate. It extended from the wall by approximately a half inch. Two bolts on either side held it securely to the wall.

He looked back at Colophon. "Just turn it?"

"Yes," she repeated. "Just turn it."

He shrugged, turned back to the wall, and tried turning the brass plate to the right.

Nothing.

He tried turning the plate to the left.

Nothing.

"It won't—"

"I know," said Colophon. "It's not budging. There has to be some sort of trigger or release."

She handed her flashlight to Julian and then walked up to the brass plate.

There wasn't much to it. It was about six inches wide, four inches high, oval in shape, with a bolt on either side.

The bolts!

Colophon placed a thumb on each bolt and, with a deep breath, pushed. For a moment, nothing happened. And then each bolt slowly started to withdraw into the wall. Once the bolts were completely withdrawn, Colophon turned the plate clockwise ninety degrees. The oval now stood upright, and the W was transformed into a Σ. Colophon stepped back from the wall.

CLICK

The sound came from within the wall.

CLICK

CLICK

"Get back," said Julian.

CLICK CLICK CLICK

Silence.

"Is that it?" asked Colophon.

The sound of metal striking metal came from behind the wall. Then in rapid succession . . . CLICK CLICK CLICK

Silence again.

Then, as they watched, the entire back wall started to move.

CLICK CLICK CLICK

The right side of the wall rotated approximately three feet into the room. The left side retreated back into a space hidden behind the wall. As it did, it revealed . . .

"A stairway!" exclaimed Colophon.

Julian and Colophon pointed their flashlights down the circular staircase, which wound into the darkness.

"Look!"

Julian pointed to an engraved plate above the staircase. Below it was a clock of some sort. And it was ticking.

The inscription on the plate read:

"It's not a clock," said Julian. "It's a timer. It appears we have exactly thirty minutes."

Colophon set the alarm on her watch to go off in thirty minutes. "And what happens if we don't get back in time?" she asked.

"I don't think we want to find out," he replied.

Julian led Colophon down the narrow stone stairway. The stairs wound in a tight circle, which prevented them from seeing more than a few feet ahead at a time. The only light came from Julian's flashlight.

He stopped suddenly and without warning. Colophon ran into his back.

"We're at the bottom," he whispered. She stepped off the last step and stood beside him. He pointed his flashlight into the darkness. It illuminated a narrow stone corridor covered in dusty cobwebs. The light tapered off into darkness. The air was thick and musty.

"Well," she said, "it looks like there's only one way to go."

"That's usually not a good thing," he noted. "Follow me." He started down the corridor. "And watch your step. There's no telling how structurally sound this corridor may be. There's an awful lot of dirt above our heads."

They moved forward slowly. After fifteen feet or so, he stopped.

"Is something the matter?" asked Colophon.

He pointed the flashlight back down the corridor.

"Look," he said.

"What?"

"Our footprints. You can see our footprints in the dust."

"So?"

"There are no other footprints in the dust. None. I think," said Julian, "that we may be the first people in this corridor . . ."

". . . in almost four hundred years," replied Colophon. "That is so cool."

The corridor ended at a small wooden door.

Julian moved the beam from his flashlight across the door and examined it carefully.

"No lock," Colophon noted.

"Perhaps Miles Letterford decided that if someone got this far, another lock would simply be overkill. However, we're not taking any chances. Stand back while I try and open it."

She took a few steps back. He reached over, grabbed the door handle, and pulled.

Nothing.

The door didn't budge.

"Hmm," said Julian. "Perhaps there's some sort of hidden lock."

"Or," said Colophon as she squeezed past her cousin, "perhaps we should simply push."

She pushed the door forward. It swung open with ease.

They entered the room beyond the wooden door. It was easily twenty feet across and at least thirty feet long. The walls were made of cut stone, and the vaulted ceiling was composed of small bricks. The whole room looked as if it could collapse at any moment.

Colophon scanned the room with her flashlight.

"Look!" She pointed her flashlight at the far end of the room.

"Remarkable!" said Julian.

Approximately five feet off the ground, on the wall at the far end of the room, was what appeared to be an exact copy of the Shakespeare monument in the church above them, albeit covered with cobwebs.

Colophon pointed her flashlight at the piece of paper held in the statue's hand. "I'll bet something's written on THAT page!" she exclaimed. "That has to be the page from the poem."

"Without a doubt," agreed Julian.

"What is this room?" asked Colophon.

"I'm not entirely sure," he replied. "But I think it may be part of the old Saxon church on top of which Holy Trinity was built."

"How is that possible? Wouldn't they have simply torn it down?"

"Not necessarily. This part of the old church may have served as a crypt or the foundation for the new church at some point. It was a fairly common practice to build churches in that manner."

"Well, no sense in waiting. Let's check out that monument," said Colophon.

"Wait."

"Why?" she asked impatiently. "We're running out of time."

"Listen."

She paused. "Why do I hear running water?" she asked.

Julian had not noticed the sound of running water when they first entered the room, but it was now unmistakable. He scanned the floor of the room with his flashlight. What he saw made his heart drop.

Colophon and Julian stood no more than ten feet from the Shakespeare monument.

It might as well have been a mile.

Approximately two feet in front of the Shakespeare monument was a gaping hole that ran directly across the room. The sound of rapidly running water rose up from somewhere deep in the hole.

"How did that get here?" asked Colophon.

"Well, the church does sit next to a river. Underground streams are certainly not uncommon."

"Do you think Miles Letterford planned this?"

Julian stared down into the hole. "I don't think so. It appears as if the floor collapsed after the monument was placed on the wall. The water probably eroded the ground underneath the floor over a period of years, and then one day—bam!—the floor was gone."

Colophon placed her hands on her hips and stared across to the monument.

"I guess it doesn't matter how it got here. The question is, how do we get across?"

Julian scanned the sides of the hole with his flashlight. On the right side of the room, a small portion of the floor remained attached to the wall. The ledge was little more than eight inches wide and, in places, substantially less.

"Perhaps," said Julian, "I could make my way along that ledge to the far side."

His voice, Colophon noted, was not brimming with confidence.

There was, however, no other way across.

"I'm smaller than you," she said. "Let me do it."

"No," he replied. "I can't allow you to do that. It's far too dangerous. And besides, your mother would kill me." He handed her the flashlight. "If anything happens to me," he said, "get out of here immediately."

"But—"

"No buts. Just leave and get help. OK?"

She looked up at him. "OK."

He took a deep breath. "All right. Now make sure you shine the flashlight so that I can see the ledge."

He tentatively tested the first foot or so of the ledge with his left foot. It appeared firm, so he scooted a little farther down the ledge. Slowly he made his way across the chasm.

Colophon glanced down at her watch. "We only have ten minutes left."

"Not a real good time for me to hurry," he huffed under his breath. "I would prefer not to get sucked into this dark underground river."

About two thirds of the way across, he stopped. He stuck his left foot out and pushed down lightly on the ledge. It crumbled into the darkness below. He was still three feet from the far side.

"I'm going to have to jump," he said.

"You don't have to," replied Colophon. "Just come back. We can find some other way."

"There's no other way. And as you said, we don't have time. I need to get over there now."

"But—"

"We don't have time," he repeated. "I have to do this."

She knew he was right.

"Be careful," she said. "You only have a foot or so of floor left on the other side."

Julian tensed his body, bent his knees, and jumped.

CHAPTER TWENTY-SIX
In the Bottom of a Tomb

Julian crashed hard against the wall and crumpled onto the small ledge.

"Are you OK?" called Colophon.

He lifted his head and peered over the edge into the darkness.

"I'm fine. Who knew that a stone wall would be so hard? Better than the alternative, I suppose."

He stood up and brushed himself off. Then he quickly made his way down to the monument.

"Well," said Colophon, "is there anything on it?"

He looked back across at her with a broad smile. "Yes."

"What does it say?"

"It says 'Ex Luna Scientia.'"

"What does that mean?" she asked.

"It means 'From the moon, knowledge.'"

"Another clue," she said, exasperated.

"Another clue," he replied. "Expecting something different?"

"A treasure map would have been nice. Now we have another problem to solve."

Julian stood by the edge and looked across at Colophon. "Actually," he said, "we now have two problems to solve. One happens to be a lot more urgent than the other—at least for the moment."

It took a second for the realization to hit Colophon.

Oh no! she thought. Julian couldn't come back the same way he had reached the monument. The ledge had started to crumble—there was no way it would hold his weight a second time.

"I'm going to have to try and jump," he said.

The gap between them seemed enormous. "You'll never make it!" she exclaimed.

"I don't have much choice, do I?" he replied. "We have to get out of here."

Colophon scanned the room with her flashlight. It was empty. She could not see anything that could be used to bridge the gap. There was only one way back across. Julian would have to jump.

"All right," she said. "You can do this."

He stepped back as far against the wall as possible and braced himself. "On the count of three," he said.

"One.

"Two.

"Three."

He took a short step and jumped. The jump was awkward, as was he. His lanky arms and legs splayed to all sides.

His right foot landed first, followed shortly thereafter by his left hand. He stood there briefly, balanced on one foot and one arm, at the edge of the hole. His left leg hung back over the abyss—his right arm was forward. He looked up at Colophon and smiled.

"And you were worried that I wouldn't make it."

The smile, however, faded quickly. He leaned backwards as his left hand came off the floor. As Colophon watched in horror, he started to pitch back into the darkness.

Palace Hotel, the basement
Wednesday, December 17, late evening

Mull Letterford sat on a metal stool, wrapped in a robe bearing the name of the hotel, with his feet soaking in a bucket filled with a mixture of baking soda, vinegar, and hydrogen peroxide. Case had found the recipe on the Internet — an all-purpose and powerful formula for odor removal — and it seemed to be working. They would probably be allowed back up into the hotel now that the smell had subsided.

Mull stared across the small utility room at his son. "Thank you," he said.

"For what?" Case asked. "I didn't do anything special. Anybody could have found a way to get rid of the smell."

"No, it's not just about the smell. I'm thanking you for being there for me today."

Case turned and looked out a small window into a storage area beyond.

"I'm sorry things didn't work out," he finally replied.

"It'll be OK. There are other authors."

Case turned back to his father. "But there aren't others. There's only one left. Isn't that true?"

His comment took Mull Letterford by surprise. "How do you know that?"

Case explained to his father how Colophon had overheard the entire conversation in the library.

"And Coly sent you here to keep an eye on me?"

"Yes," he replied.

Mull laughed. "You didn't have to go to the museum, did you?"

"No. I'm sorry. I know you're probably mad at me." Case's eyes were tinged with red.

"Mad at you?" Mull replied. "How could I be mad at you? You came here to help me—to help the family business. I couldn't be prouder of you than I am right now."

"But what if they take everything away from you—from us?"

Mull stepped out of the bucket and walked over to his son.

"It doesn't matter. Really. As long as I have my family, that's the only thing that matters. That's what's real."

Case reached over and hugged his father. "You're not going to tell Coly about this, are you? It could ruin my reputation as the mean older brother."

"Not a chance."

"Thanks, Dad."

Mull sat back down, grabbed a towel, and started drying his feet.

"You know," said Case, "Coly has a theory about why all this bad stuff has happened lately."

"And the theory is?"

"She thinks some guy named Tree-something is behind all this."

Mull leaned back and looked up at the ceiling. "Treemont," he said.

"That's the name. I told her she was crazy, but you know Coly."

"I don't think your sister's crazy."

"You mean it's possible he did all of this?"

"Yes," Mull replied. "I think it's entirely possible."

"So what did you do to get this guy mad at you?"

Mull paused. "I was born," he finally replied. "He's my second cousin, and he has always resented the fact that the company was going to be passed down to me."

"Wow—this guy Treemont is your cousin?"

"Yes, but don't let that fool you. Family means nothing to him."

Case turned back around and stared out the window. "Dad, have you always wanted to own Letterford and Sons?"

"Hardly," Mull said. "When I was your age, I had no

interest whatsoever in running a publishing house. I mean, what self-respecting fifteen-year-old would?"

The answer caught Case off guard. He had assumed that his father had always wanted to run the company.

"So what changed your mind?" he asked.

"I simply realized at some point that running the company wasn't an obligation, it was a privilege. I was born a Letterford, but I made the choice to be part of Letterford and Sons—no one forced me." He paused. "And when the time comes, it will be your decision and your decision only."

"Promise?" replied Case. He had never thought of it as a choice he could make—he had always viewed his birthright as a burden.

"Promise," replied Mull.

Then he looked at his son. "I have a question to ask you." His voice took on a serious tone. "Did my feet actually make someone throw up?"

Case grinned. "All over the floor in the elevator lobby."

Stratford-upon-Avon
Wednesday, December 17

Colophon seized Julian's jacket and held fast. She

could feel herself being pulled forward into the crack with him.

"Let go!" he yelled. "You can't hold me!"

Colophon stared into Julian's eyes.

"I . . . WILL . . . NOT . . . LET . . . GO!"

Colophon threw all her weight backwards in one swift motion. She and Julian tumbled backwards and landed with a thump on the stone floor.

"You're stronger than you look," said Julian.

"And you're heavier than you look," said Colophon, as she stood up. Her whole backside ached from falling on the stone floor and from serving as a landing pad for Julian.

She glanced down at the illuminated dials on her watch.

"Run!" she cried. They now had thirty seconds to reach the door before it slammed shut.

Flashlight forward, they scampered quickly across the room and through the door into the hallway.

CLICK . . . CLICK . . . CLICK

The clicking noise echoed down the hallway.

CLICK—CLICK—CLICK—CLICK—CLICK

The pace of the clicks increased as they sped down the hallway and started up the stairs.

CLICK CLICK CLICK CLICK CLICK CLICK CLICK CLICK

Julian made the final turn first and burst through the opening. As Colophon put her foot on the final step, she tripped and fell forward. Her flashlight fell from her hands, hit the wall, and rolled back down the stairs. As she watched, the light from the flashlight bounced against the wall of the stairs and then was gone. The alarm on her watch started beeping. The clicking had stopped.

"Julian!" she cried.

As soon as Julian made it through the door and into the mausoleum, he heard the thud behind him and Colophon's cry. He turned back to the door. It was slowly closing.

Colophon tried to get to her knees, but she felt as if she were moving in slow motion. The light from Julian's flashlight illuminated the opening into the mausoleum, but it was growing dimmer. The stone door was starting to shut. Suddenly the light was gone.

She was trapped.

Julian threw down his flashlight and thrust his arms back through the narrowing opening. He groped around for Colophon. Nothing.

Where was she?

Colophon was scrambling on her knees in the direction of the door, or at least where she thought the door was.

It was so dark

Was the door already closed?

Suddenly something grabbed her right hand.

This was no time to be delicate. As soon as he felt it, Julian grabbed her hand and pulled. Her feet barely made it past the stone door before it slammed shut. The sounds of metal bolts locking into place— for the final time—rang through the cold and dark mausoleum.

Julian and Colophon sat on the floor. Despite the cold, they were covered in sweat.

"You know, you're stronger than you look," said Colophon.

Julian paused and caught his breath. "And you're heavier than you appear," replied Julian.

They both laughed nervously. The laughter, however, ended quickly as the room filled with light and a deep voice from behind them announced: "What 'r you doing in here?"

CHAPTER TWENTY-SEVEN
Of Other Men's Secrets

Colophon and Julian stood in front of Reverend Mackey's large oak desk in the church. Behind them stood the graveyard's caretaker—Charlie Thompson—a man of considerable size and girth, whose flattened face matched his grim demeanor.

Reverend Mackey leaned back in his chair. "I was in the middle of watching a terrific match between

Northampton and Worcester, in front of a very warm fire with a nice brandy, when Mr. Thompson telephoned to inform me that he had found some trespassers in one of the mausoleums."

"Just sittin' there, they were," added the caretaker, "right in the middle of the bloody mausoleum. I saw the light from their flashlight under the door. I knew I had caught me some trespassers, I did."

"This is not," the reverend continued, "the first time we have had a break-in. It seems to be a favorite rite of passage for much of the youth in this area. I was, however, shocked to learn that the trespassers this evening were members of the respected Letterford family. Quite a catch, I must say. Mr. Thompson certainly does an excellent job of keeping an eye on the grounds."

Charlie Thompson puffed out his chest in pride. "Thank you, sir. I do my best, I do. Now, shall I ring for the constable?"

Colophon and Julian looked at Reverend Mackey.

"No," the reverend replied.

The air instantly went out of Charlie Thompson's chest. "But sir? These two—"

"Thank you, Mr. Thompson. You have done an excellent job this evening, but I believe I will handle this particular matter myself."

The caretaker shrugged his broad shoulders, grunted a brief goodbye, and then departed the room.

"I sincerely apologize," said Julian. "This is all my fault. I should never—"

Reverend Mackey held up his hand. Julian stopped speaking.

"You know," the reverend said, "you gave Mr. Thompson quite a start this evening. He's a superstitious sort. There's no telling what was going through his head."

"Are you going to call the police?" asked Colophon.

"Ah, now that is the question, isn't it?" replied Reverend Mackey. "As you are probably aware, the mausoleums are private property. They are not open to the public. That's why they have locks." He shot a glance at Julian.

"Anyway," the reverend continued, "only people authorized by the family are permitted to enter a mausoleum. There are no exceptions. To enter a mausoleum without permission is considered trespassing—not to mention bad taste."

This was it. Colophon was headed for jail. How could she explain this to her mother?

"Again," Julian interrupted, "I must accept full responsibility. I am the adult. The girl was only following me."

Reverend Mackey looked over at Colophon. "Is that true?"

She looked down at her shoes. "No," she replied in a low voice. "I can't let Julian accept the blame. It was my idea."

"I see," said Reverend Mackey. "Well, I guess my hands are tied on this matter."

"So you're calling the police?" asked Colophon.

"No."

"No?" repeated Julian.

"No."

"But I thought only authorized—"

"That is correct," said Reverend Mackey. "Only those who are authorized may enter the mausoleum. However, as odd and coincidental as it may seem, it appears that descendants of Miles Letterford are specifically authorized to access that particular mausoleum."

Colophon and Julian stared at the reverend in disbelief.

"Authorized? But how?" she asked.

"Authorized by the man who built and paid for the mausoleum," replied Reverend Mackey. "Miles Letterford himself."

Of course! Colophon thought.

"And so," continued Reverend Mackey, "although

the hour you choose to access the mausoleum was, shall we say . . . unusual, you were quite authorized to do so. And so, with that, I think I will be getting back to the match I was watching when I was interrupted."

Julian and Colophon stood up.

"I do want to apologize for any inconvenience we have caused," said Julian.

"Think nothing of it," replied Reverend Mackey. "Part of the job, I suppose."

Reverend Mackey walked around the desk and shook Julian's hand. He then turned to Colophon and extended his hand.

"It has been a pleasure, young Miss Letterford."

Charlie Thompson had been the caretaker of the graveyard at Holy Trinity for fifteen years, and he took his job very seriously. Over the years, he had run off hundreds of teenagers, drunk university students, and other assorted miscreants. He once found a cow dressed as a matador grazing among the graves. As such, the evening's events were not particularly unusual. Even so, Charlie realized that there was something different about the young girl and her disheveled cousin.

They were not teenagers walking through the graveyard on a dare.

They were not inebriated university students.

And they most certainly did not fit into the general miscreant category.

No, this was different.

Charlie pulled out his wallet and retrieved a small card from it. A phone number was printed on the card—nothing else. He stared at the number for a moment and then stuffed it back into his wallet.

It wouldn't be right, he thought.

He paced along the stone path outside the door to the church. *But would it be wrong?*

It was just a little extra money.

Nothing wrong with that at all.

Besides, it wasn't like anyone was going to get hurt.

After pacing for several minutes, he stopped. He had made up his mind. He retrieved the card from his wallet and dialed the number.

The phone rang twice.

"Yes?" a voice answered.

"Yes . . . uh . . . sir, this is Charlie Thompson. I work at the church in Stratford. I don't know if you remember me?"

"I remember you," the voice replied.

"Well, sir, you said you would make it worth my while to call you if anything strange happened—you know, not the usual strange—something strange strange."

"And something of the sort has happened?"

"I should say so," replied Charlie.

"Then, my friend, I will make it worth your while to share that information with me."

Charlie explained the events of the evening in considerable detail, if not in complete chronological order.

"And what were the names of the vandals who broke into the mausoleum?" the voice asked.

"I didn't quite catch their first names, sir, but the last name stuck with me—Letterford. Not a name you hear much, you know?"

There was no response. Charlie looked at his cell phone to make sure the call was still active. "Sir? Are you still there?"

"Yes," the voice finally replied, "I am still here. You have done well, my friend. I assure you that Mrs. Thompson will be able to enjoy a splendid vacation in Bournemouth this summer."

"Thank you, sir," Charlie replied. "But there's one more thing."

"Yes?"

"Well, sir, it's just that I could've sworn I heard a door slam before I entered the mausoleum. I know that doesn't make any sense—there's no door in that mausoleum 'cepting the one I opened."

"Of course there wasn't another door," the voice said calmly. "You know how these old structures are —particularly at night. They make the strangest sounds."

"Well," Charlie muttered, "I suppose you're right. It's been a long day. Anyway, the missus will sure appreciate the vacation."

"I am sure she will," replied the voice. "I am sure she will."

The line clicked, and the call was over.

There—that wasn't so bad, was it? Charlie thought.

New York City

Trigue James closed his cell phone and sat back to contemplate the news he had just received.

The Letterfords had made it to Stratford.

James was impressed. Treemont's intuition had been correct—someone from the family had shown up at the church snooping around. Treemont had instructed James to have someone keep an eye on the church—"just in case," he had said. It had seemed like a waste of time, and James had been extremely doubtful that anything would happen. After all, Treemont had never explained exactly why someone would show up at the church or what they would be looking for, and James had never asked. It wasn't wise to ask too many questions in his line of work.

Still, James could not help but wonder. The connection between the church and Treemont's efforts to take over the publishing company were not clear. *Curious.*

But, James realized, that was a curiosity to be explored some other day. Right now he had to determine exactly what they had found at the church, if anything. He opened his laptop and started booking his flight to London. He would call Treemont on the way to the airport.

M40 Motorway
Wednesday, December 17, late evening

"I know where we're supposed to go next!" Colophon blurted out as soon as she got into the car to return to London.

"But of course you do," replied Julian. "I'm starting to get used to it. Well, don't leave me waiting."

"The moon. The moon is the clue!"

"Duh," replied Julian. "I got that far. After all, that's what the clue says—'from the moon, knowledge.'"

"No. I know *which* moon," corrected Colophon.

"There is more than one?"

"Actually, there are many," replied Colophon, "but only one in our house."

"What are you talking about?"

"I just knew that I had seen the silver globe in Miles Letterford's portrait before, but I couldn't figure out where. Now I know. It's part of the tellurion in our library. The silver globe in the painting is the moon in the tellurion in the Letterford library!"

CHAPTER TWENTY-EIGHT
Swifter than the Wandering Moon

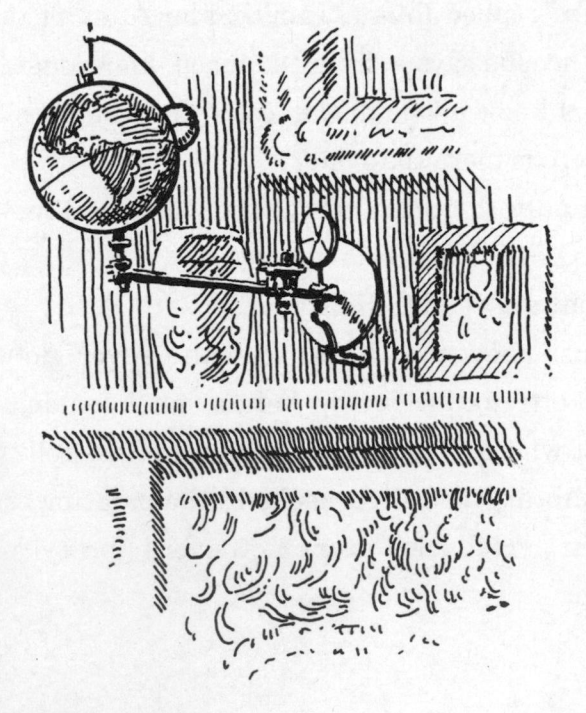

The Grand Library
London
Thursday, December 18
9:00 a.m.

Julian and Colophon stood in front of the tellurion in the library in London. Mounted above the fireplace, it appeared—at first glance—to be some sort of odd, misshapen clock. A large concave brass plate sat in the middle of the spectacular contraption and represented the sun. The earth—represented by a copper globe (which had oxidized over time into a soft green color) engraved with the latin term *terra*—was connected to the brass plate representing the sun by a sturdy brass rod. The moon—a small silver globe engraved with the latin term *luna*—was attached to the earth by means of another brass rod. The brass rods were, in turn, connected to the earth and moon in such a manner as to allow each sphere to rotate as it would in its natural orbit around the sun.

"I thought the tellurion was in Manchester," said Colophon. "Isn't this just a copy?"

"Actually," replied Julian, "*this* is the original. It's one of the few items from Miles's library that was not transported to America. Apparently it's bolted to the stone mantel in such a way that it cannot be removed without ripping out the entire works—which, if you think about it, is a bit of good luck for us, since we're in London and not Manchester."

"I don't think luck has anything to do with it," said Colophon. I think Miles Letterford wanted that machine to stay right where it is."

Julian nodded in agreement. "That would make

sense. And the moon is certainly an appropriate clue—very Shakespearean. The moon was practically a character in a couple of his plays."

"Are you going to quote Shakespeare again?"

Julian smiled. "I am considering it."

"OK," replied Colophon, "let's get it over with."

Julian turned to her and took a short bow. "Thank you—here goes:

"'We the globe can compass soon,

Swifter than the wandering moon.'"

"Nice," replied Colophon. "Are you done?"

"Yes—and for the record, I spent half the night trying to memorize it."

Julian turned back toward the tellurion. "Actually, I was hoping there would be something in one of Shakespeare's works that might help us—some clue. I came up with nothing but that quote. Unfortunately, we're still left with the same question that has dogged us throughout this search—what next?"

Colophon pointed to a large brass box with a series of dials at the base of the tellurion. "I think we're supposed to enter a date and see what happens."

"OK, that makes sense," replied Julian. "But what date? Miles Letterford's birthday? The date the company was founded? The date of his firstborn child? There are so many possibilities!"

"Well," said Colophon, "all the clues we've discovered so far have in some way looped back on one another."

"How so?"

"Think about it—the painting in Manchester led us to the Shakespeare Monument in Stratford. The poem on the monument led us to a hidden copy of the monument under the church. The clue on that monument led us back to the painting, which led us to here."

Julian nodded. "True, but where are we looping back to this time? I hope you aren't suggesting that we need to go back to the church? I have a yearly limit on near-death experiences, and I'm maxed out for this year."

"That won't be necessary," replied Colophon.

Julian paused and looked up at the tellurion and then at Colophon. "There's no need to go back because you already know what we're looking for, don't you?"

Colophon grinned proudly. "Yes, as a matter of fact I believe I do."

"And you were planning to keep me waiting for how long?"

"Oh, very well," said Colophon. "The date we're looking for is obviously the date of Shakespeare's death—April 23, 1616. I knew the year he died from his grave, but not the day or month. I looked up the full date online last night. That has to be the answer!"

"Ahh," said Julian, "so we loop back to the church itself? But why the date of his death and not his birth? April twenty-third was also the day he was born in 1564. Remember, he was baptized in the same church in which he is buried."

The grin never left Colophon's face. Julian realized immediately that she had already thought through this possibility.

"Because the clues were the monument and the mausoleum," she noted.

"Of course," said Julian. "And those clues relate to his death, not his birth."

"Exactly!" she replied.

He pulled over a small stool and put it in front of the tellurion. "Madam," he said, bending forward with a flourish of his arm, "you should have the honor."

Colophon stepped up onto the stool and carefully turned the knobs on the tellurion.

The knob for the day, she set at twenty-three.

For the month—April.

There were two knobs for the year. The first she

set to the number sixteen. The second she likewise set to the number sixteen.

She gave the key on the side of the box three turns to the right and then released it.

The key slowly started to unwind.

Colophon stepped off the stool and went back to Julian's side.

Nothing happened at first.

Then three loud clicks.

CLICK CLICK CLICK

Julian backed away from the tellurion. "You know, I'm really not a fan of things that go 'click' since our incident in the graveyard."

CLICK . . . Click . . . click.

Colophon took three steps back. "Good point," she replied.

click . . . click

Suddenly, the silver globe started rotating counterclockwise around the copper globe. Then—with a jerk—it stopped.

Another moment or so passed.

CLICK . . .

Finally, the copper globe—the earth—started to move smoothly around the brass plate representing the sun. The silver orb representing the moon started moving once again around the earth.

Julian and Colophon waited several minutes as the earth slowly encircled the sun. When the earth had made one full rotation, it stopped, as did the moon.

And then nothing.

Colophon and Julian looked at each other, perplexed.

Then three soft clicks:

click, click, click.

They looked back up at the tellurion.

click, click, click.

"I can't tell where the clicking sound is coming from," Colophon said, "but it doesn't seem to be the same place as before."

click, click, whirrrrrrrrrr . . . click.

She stepped back up on the stool.

"Be careful," he said.

"The noise," she replied. "It's coming from the moon."

Julian moved closer to the tellurion.

click, click.

Suddenly, the top of the small silver orb opened and rotated forward.

"C'mon, c'mon, I can't see with you standing there," exclaimed Julian. "What's in it?"

Colophon grinned, looked down at Julian, and held

aloft a small gold object for him to see. "I believe," she said, "that it is a key."

Colophon placed the gold object on the kitchen table. Julian pulled a small magnifying glass from inside his coat and bent over to examine it. It was definitely a key, approximately two inches long and gold or gold plated. Stamped into the end of the key was the outline of a fish, and inside the fish was stamped the word BARTWICK.

"Bartwick?" she asked as she looked over his shoulder. "What is a Bartwick? Is that another clue?"

Julian sat back in his chair. He pulled his glasses off and started cleaning them with a handkerchief from his pocket.

"Well?" asked Colophon.

He put his glasses back on and looked at her. "Do you know what this mark is?" he asked.

"I have no idea," she said.

Julian pumped his fist in the air. "Finally," he exclaimed, "I know something that my twelve-year-old second cousin does not!"

He held up the key. "After graduating from college with a degree in sixteenth-century Lithuanian literature, I discovered, to my surprise, that there weren't a lot of job opportunities in that particular field. I managed, however, to secure a job as a researcher for a London auction house. Among the items I researched were gold boxes, silverware, and other small but valuable trinkets. I saw this type of mark all the time—it's a maker's mark. It was placed on this key by the goldsmith who made it."

"A goldsmith?"

"Yes, someone who worked with gold, and perhaps silver and other metals as well. The mark was required by the goldsmith's guild so that people would know who made the object and to testify to its quality."

"So Bartwick is not a thing? It's a who?"

"Yes, a who. Bartwick—or more precisely Percy Bartwick—was a well-known goldsmith back in the time of Miles Letterford."

"So, how does that help us?"

"Well, suppose you had something very valuable back in the early seventeenth century. Where would you keep it?"

"The bank?"

"There were no banks back then. So where else?"

"I'm guessing the goldsmith?"

"Exactly," replied Julian. "Security was extremely important for a goldsmith, as you might imagine. After all, they worked with gold. Because of this, goldsmiths would keep valuable objects for customers—for a fee of course."

"I don't suppose," said Colophon, "that there's any chance that this particular goldsmith is still in business after four hundred years?"

"Oh, most certainly not. I am confident that Bartwick the goldsmith died centuries ago."

Colophon sighed dejectedly. "So we *have* hit another wall."

Julian peered over his glasses at her and grinned.

"Care for a walk about London this afternoon?" he asked.

London
Thursday, December 18
11:00 a.m.

"Coly!" yelled Mrs. Letterford. "It's your brother on the phone. He needs to speak with you."

Colophon sprinted down the stairs, grabbed the cordless phone from her mother, and headed for the dining room.

"You're up early," she said. "What is it, five o'clock in the morning in Manchester?"

"Don't remind me," Case responded.

"So," she continued, "how did it go in New York?"

Case let out a short laugh. "Go get your laptop and then come back to the phone." Colophon put down the phone and raced upstairs to retrieve her laptop.

Once back downstairs, she opened it up and grabbed the phone. "I have it in front of me."

Case told his sister to go to YouTube and search for a video labeled "Dog Day in New York."

There was silence on the phone for several moments.

"Oh, no!" she exclaimed.

"Yeah," Case answered.

"Has Dad seen this?"

"Not yet," replied Case.

"Oh, no."

"Yeah, I got that the first time," Case said. "So tell me, Sherlock, have you solved the mystery yet?"

Case's sarcasm usually drove Colophon nuts, but something in his voice seemed different this time. He seemed more good-natured—less mean. "I'm getting there," she replied. She spent the next ten minutes describing the events of the prior day.

Not bad, Case thought when his little sister finished. *Not bad at all.*

Trigue James was equally impressed by Colophon and what she had found. He had listened to the conversation between Colophon and Case from the relative comfort of his rental car, parked across the street from the Letterford home in London. It had been easy enough to listen in on the call, particularly since the Letterfords insisted on using a cordless phone and not a landline. James simply had to dial into the correct frequency, and *voilà*, instant access to the Letterfords' private conversations.

James texted a short message to Treemont: "They have a key." Then he sat back in his seat, sipped his coffee, and waited. A moment later his phone pinged. The text back from Treemont was equally short and concise: *"Get it."*

CHAPTER THIRTY
With Golden Promises

London
Thursday, December 18
2:05 p.m.

The cold London air and a chilling mist enveloped
Colophon and Julian as they made their way along

the crowded streets of London. They walked for several blocks in silence, their frosty breaths trailing behind them. Suddenly, Julian stopped.

"Why have we stopped?" asked Colophon.

"This is the intersection of Bishopsgate and Threadneedle Street," said Julian as he turned and gestured at the cross streets in front of them. "Threadneedle Street used to be—as the name suggests—the street where you could find a good tailor. It's now the heart of London's financial district. The Bank of England is located just down this street. Millions of people entrust the financial institutions here to take care of their most valuable financial assets. But as we discussed this morning, when Miles Letterford was alive, there were no banks."

"Yes," Colophon said, "and people used goldsmiths to protect their treasures. But what does that have to do with where we are now? This wasn't the goldsmiths' district."

Julian gestured for her to follow as he proceeded down Threadneedle Street. "It's true that there were no banks and that this was not the goldsmiths' district. Goldsmiths, however, had to be very careful. The items that they worked on were valuable. So they had to develop ways of protecting them from thieves and burglars. Out of necessity, they became very good at doing just that. Many goldsmiths soon discovered that it was more profitable to hold items of value for a fee than to produce gold objects."

Colophon stopped. "Wait," she said, "are you trying to tell me that the goldsmiths became—"

"Banks," interjected Julian. "Not all of them, of course. There are still goldsmiths. But yes, that is essentially how many of the banks in England were founded."

Julian then pointed to the building in front of where they had stopped.

"This is B and C Bank of London," he said. "Care to guess what the B in B and C stands for?"

"Bartwick!" exclaimed Colophon.

"Exactly," replied Julian. "B and C Bank of London, or more formally, Bartwick and Cavendish Bank of London."

Colophon patted the pocket in which she had placed the key prior to leaving the house. "Do you think that they would still have whatever this key opens?"

"Well, my dear, there is only one way to find out. Shall we cross the street and go see?"

Trigue James had followed Colophon and Julian as they left the Letterford home and now watched from across the street as they entered the bank. A quick Internet search on his phone told him everything he needed to know about the bank—private institution, rich clientele, world-class security, and a reputation for strict confidentiality. This would not be easy.

James knew he didn't have much time, but he had already started formulating a plan. Fortunately, he knew people—people who would do anything if they got paid and who had rather unique skills.

He dialed a number on his cell phone. The phone rang twice and was picked up on the other end. James did not introduce himself. "I have a job for you," he said.

Colophon and Julian entered the lobby of the bank through a pair of large, ornate brass doors. The lobby—such as it was—did not appear anything like the banks she had been to in America. In the middle of the room was a small glass desk, behind which sat an extremely proper-looking middle-aged woman. There was no other furniture in the room.

"This doesn't look like a bank," whispered Colophon.

"It's a private bank," replied Julian. "It serves a

very limited number of select customers. In many ways, it still operates much like the goldsmith who founded it."

"May I help you?" the receptionist interrupted. Her tone was pleasant but matter-of-fact.

"Ah," replied Julian, "is there a banker with whom we may speak?"

She looked at Julian and then at Colophon, and then back at Julian. "Do you have an appointment?"

"No," replied Julian.

"I'm terribly sorry," she said. "Our bankers meet with customers by appointment *only*." Colophon noted that the tone of this statement was decidedly cooler, and she most certainly did not sound "terribly sorry." "If you will leave me your name and contact number," she continued, "I will have someone call you at their earliest convenience."

Colophon bristled at the receptionist's tone. She knew that they were running out of time. She took out the key and placed it on the receptionist's desk. "We need to speak with someone about this immediately," she said.

The receptionist picked up the key and examined it. She offered no indication as to whether she recognized it. Her outward demeanor did not change.

"Please wait," she said. The receptionist then exited through a door hidden in the panels of the wall behind her desk, taking the key with her.

Colophon and Julian stood in the lobby. The only sound was the faint *whoosh* of the heated air as it entered the room through vents in the white marble floor. The receptionist returned moments later and took her seat. "Someone will be with you shortly," she said. No other commentary or explanation was offered.

Finally, after almost five minutes, a door in the wall to their left opened, and a proper-looking older gentleman in a pinstriped gray suit entered the room. The man stood ramrod straight, with a shock of white hair on top of his head. Dark, thick-rimmed glasses sat on the end of his nose.

"Good day," he said in a pleasant manner. "I am Walter Davenport. I am in charge of the stored assets collection. Would you care to follow me?"

Julian and Colophon followed Mr. Davenport through the door, down a short nondescript hallway, up a short flight of stairs, and into an office overlooking Threadneedle Street. He directed Julian and Colophon to a set of chairs in front of a large oak desk. The room was devoid of anything other than three chairs and the desk. Nothing on the walls. No bookshelves. And nothing on the desk except for a single folder. Colophon could make out the word on top of the folder—LETTERFORD.

Mr. Davenport sat in a chair behind the desk and peered over his glasses at Julian and Colophon. "And with whom do I have the pleasure of speaking this afternoon?"

"My name is Colophon Letterford, and this is my cousin, Julian Letterford."

"Very good," replied Mr. Davenport. "That offers at least a partial response to my next question."

"Which is?" asked Julian.

"How you happened to come into possession of this particular object?" Davenport placed the key on the envelope on his desk.

"It belongs to my family. Do you know what it is?" asked Colophon.

"I should say so," replied Davenport.

"And what is it? What does it open?"

"In due course, Ms. Letterford, in due course. As you may know, we are a private bank. We maintain a strict code of protecting both our clients' assets and their privacy. I don't mean to be disrespectful, but we normally don't hand over information to people simply because they show up with a key with our name on it."

Davenport paused. He ran his fingers across the key.

"This is not," Davenport continued, "a normal situation, is it?"

He did not wait for a response.

"We have, for centuries, maintained and protected our customers' most treasured assets—many in safe boxes. Once someone has purchased a safe box from our firm, it is that person's property forever. We, in turn, are obligated to secure that box forever. We have several safe boxes that are extremely old. None, however, are older than one particular box."

Davenport held up the key.

"This is the key that opens that particular box."

"What's in the box?" asked Colophon.

"I have no idea," replied Davenport. "My job is to protect the box and its contents. What it contains is of no relevance to me. That particular box has remained locked for almost four hundred years. I doubt that there is a living soul who knows what it contains."

"Can I open it?" asked Colophon excitedly. "I have the key."

"I am afraid not," replied Davenport. "According to the registration documents"—Davenport patted the envelope on his desk—"the only person authorized to access the box is the owner of Letterford & Sons, and no one else."

"But my father—"

"Is not here, is he?" responded Davenport, politely but firmly.

Chapter Thirty-One
Foul Deeds Will Rise

B&C Bank of London, the lobby
London

Beatrix Rutherford sat at her desk in the lobby of B&C Bank of London. The unexpected appearance of the young girl with the key had caused a great deal of excitement in the bank's back rooms. No one, however, had bothered to explain to her what the excitement was all about—they never did, of course. Secrecy was the first principle of the bank—if you didn't need to know, you weren't told.

Beatrix's musings were interrupted by the chime of the bank door.

She looked up to see a man entering. He shook the rain off his umbrella and placed it in the brass umbrella stand by the door.

Beatrix took a quick, almost imperceptible, glance at the scheduling calendar on the computer screen built into her desk—there were no appointments scheduled for another two hours.

"I'm terribly sorry," the man said as he approached the receptionist's desk, "but I am looking for the offices of Smith and Bickward. I have an appointment in ten minutes."

Beatrix looked out through the front window at the sign for Smith and Bickward across the street. She suppressed her natural inclination to offer a smart comment. It was, she understood, not appropriate for a person in her position.

"Smith and Bickward is located immediately

across the street," she replied in her polite but firm voice. "There is a sign on the door."

"Thank you so much," the man replied as he turned and departed.

Later, when asked to describe the man, all Beatrix could remember was that he wore thick-rimmed glasses and a broad-brimmed bucket hat. She didn't know what color hair he had, how tall he was, his approximate age, or whether he spoke with an accent. Nothing stood out—she had not even noticed that he failed to retrieve his umbrella as he left.

Threadneedle Street
London

Trigue James walked half a block from the bank before removing the glasses and the hat. He deposited them in the nearest garbage can. He next removed his coat—a rain jacket with reversible lining—and turned it inside out. He knew that he could walk back into the bank right now, and the receptionist wouldn't recognize him.

But that wasn't his plan.

"Only your father can access the box," Davenport reiterated. "Is he, by any chance, in London?"

"No," replied Colophon, "and he won't arrive until late on Christmas Eve."

She slumped into her chair.

Julian stood up from his chair and walked over to the window overlooking Threadneedle Street. "I want to apologize for so rudely interrupting your day without an appointment," he said. "You have been quite helpful."

"Thank you. It was not an inconvenience at all," replied Davenport. "Quite fascinating, in fact."

Julian turned toward Davenport. "May I ask one last question?"

"Please," replied Davenport.

"Is the owner of the box required to open it here at your office?"

Davenport paused briefly. "No," he finally replied. "It has long been our practice to accommodate our customers in whatever manner necessary."

Julian continued to stare out the window. "Then perhaps I might make a simple request?"

"Of course."

Davenport listened intently to Julian's request. When Julian had finished, Davenport sat silently for several moments in deep thought. "I believe," he finally replied, "that we may be able to accommodate that particular request."

Davenport reached into his coat pocket and pulled out a small black case. Engraved on top of the case was the bank's name. Davenport placed the key in the case, closed it gently, and handed it to Colophon. "Take great care of this key, dear girl."

Colophon placed the case in her shoulder bag and slung it over her shoulder. "Don't worry," she said. "It's not going anywhere."

Trigue James stood across the street from the bank. He dialed a number on his phone, waited, and then pushed the pound symbol. Within seconds, smoke was pouring from the front of the bank. James turned and walked down Threadneedle Street, away from the bank.

Davenport was in the process of escorting Julian and Colophon back to the lobby when the alarm sounded. They all stopped in midstep. Several bank employees stuck their heads out of their offices to see what was happening.

"Don't worry," said Davenport reassuringly. "It's probably just a false alarm. I don't believe we had a drill planned for today."

But then they noticed the smoke coming from under the door leading into the lobby.

"Fire!" someone yelled, and panic ensued. Employees poured out of offices and headed for the back of the building. The hallway was suddenly packed with people.

Colophon noticed that even in the middle of all the chaos, Davenport remained calm. "We have an emergency exit in the back of the building," he said. "Please follow me."

Colophon and Julian followed Davenport down a short hallway. They turned right and then back to the left to a steel door leading to the alley behind the bank. The alley was packed with bank employees. Colophon could already hear the distinctive sirens of the London Fire Brigade headed their way.

Davenport pointed down the alley. "We need to make our way to the street," he said. The crowd, seemingly acting on Davenport's instructions, moved collectively in that direction. Colophon held tight to her bag with her right hand as she was bumped and jostled from all sides, and she grasped Julian's arm with her left. She could now see the alley opening into the street beyond. At least one fire truck had already arrived, and a crowd had gathered to watch. Just as she was about to push her way out of the alley, however, Colophon felt a jerk on her right arm.

She looked down. Her bag was gone. In front of her, a man in a dark suit was walking quickly out of the alley with her bag in his hand.

"He took my bag!" Colophon screamed at Julian. "He took the key!"

Chapter Thirty-Two
This Chase is Hotly Follow'd

Threadneedle Street
London

Followed closely by Colophon, Julian pushed his way through the crowd and burst out of the alley onto

Threadneedle Street. Chaos was everywhere. Sirens blared, and lights flashed. Firemen ran up and down the sidewalk. Smoke poured from the front of the building. A large crowd had gathered to take in all the excitement.

Colophon pointed at a man in a dark suit walking quickly down the sidewalk and away from the crowd. "There he is!" she exclaimed.

Julian and Colophon took off in pursuit. The man turned and glanced back at the crowd. When he saw Colophon and Julian gaining on him, he broke into a sprint and rounded the next corner.

Colophon and Julian turned the corner just in time to see the man closing the back door of a taxi, which sped off. In seconds the taxi reached the end of the block and turned left. It was gone, as was the key.

From the back of his taxi, Nick Davies dialed his cell phone.

"I got it," he said. "Like I told you—no problems. The smoke was a nice touch, though. I'll meet you directly opposite the Lido at Hyde Park in, say, thirty minutes?"

Davies ended the call and leaned back in his seat.

✦　✦　✦

Colophon and Julian walked slowly back to the bank.

"It's over," Colophon said. "That's it. No key, no box."

"Maybe the bank could open the box without the key," replied Julian. He did not sound confident.

By the time they reached the bank, the crowd had started to disperse, and only one fire truck remained. Davenport stood outside the front door speaking with a fireman. When he saw Colophon and Julian, he excused himself and walked over.

"I must apologize for the inconvenience," said Davenport. "It was a false alarm. A prankster set off some sort of smoke bomb in the lobby." He then noticed that Colophon appeared upset. "Is everything all right?"

"A man stole my bag!" she cried. "It had the key in it. It's gone!"

"I see," replied Davenport.

"Can the box be opened without the key?" asked Julian.

"Why certainly," replied Davenport cheerily. "No one could be expected to hold on to a key forever."

Colophon and Julian looked at each excitedly. There was still a chance this would work.

"However," Davenport continued, "it takes a minimum of two weeks to complete the paperwork and have a new key cast."

The hope drained from Colophon's face. "So it's over," she said. Julian grabbed her hand and held tight.

Colophon looked up and noticed that Davenport had a slight smile on his face.

Smiling? she thought. How could he smile at a time like this?

"Over?" said Davenport. "Hardly." He pulled a cell phone out of his vest pocket and dialed a number. "Excuse me for a moment." He walked a few feet away to speak on the phone. He returned moments later, the phone safely back in his vest pocket. "The sun seems to be peeking through the clouds," he said. "Perfect weather for a brief sightseeing tour of London, wouldn't you agree?"

Hyde Park
London

Nick Davies sat on a bench overlooking the Serpentine, the long man-made lake at Hyde Park. Across the water was the Lido, the park's popular summer swimming area. Davies checked his watch.

He should be here any minute.

But Davies was in no rush. It had been a clean getaway. No one had caught a good look at his face. He had discarded the girl's purse several blocks from the park, and he could feel the weight of the key case in his coat pocket. He had pulled off the job like the professional he was. He was, as far as anyone in the park knew, simply an anonymous Londoner enjoying the view of the lake.

Davies sipped his tea and watched several ducks swim back and forth on the lake.

Not a bad day, he thought.

Davies's reverie was interrupted by an older gentleman in a pinstriped gray suit. "Is this seat taken?" the man asked.

Davies nodded at the empty end of the bench. "All yours," he replied.

The man sat on the far end of the bench. "I really hate to bother you," said the older gentleman, "but may I ask a favor?"

"Pardon?" said Davies.

"A favor." repeated the older gentleman. "May I ask a favor?"

Davies made a mental note to steal the man's wallet before he left the park. "Sure," he replied.

"May I have the key back?"

The question startled Davies. Had the old goat just asked for a key?

"The key," the man repeated. "May I have the key you stole?"

Davies started to deny any knowledge of any key when a uniformed police officer suddenly appeared behind the older gentleman. Davies looked around. Four other police officers were now in the immediate vicinity. He had nowhere to run. Davies contemplated briefly whether he should attempt to escape by jumping in the lake. The older gentleman gave a slight smile. "The key?" he simply said.

Davies sighed, pulled the black case from his coat pocket, and handed it over.

"Thank you," Davenport said.

Davenport handed Colophon the black case. She had been convinced that she would never see it again—that the key was gone forever. Her hands trembled slightly as she opened the case and looked at the key inside. "Thank you," she said.

"Not necessary," replied Davenport. "Simply part of the job."

"But how were you able to do this?" asked Julian.

"Modern technology is wonderful. The case has a

tracking device in it. I simply activated the device and notified the police. The case has been beaming its GPS coordinates ever since."

"But why did he steal the case?" asked Colophon.

"Apparently the gentleman who stole your bag is a well-known pickpocket," replied Davenport. "The police think you were simply in the wrong place at the wrong time. They suspect he set off the smoke bomb, but they can't prove it."

"And do you think I was simply in the wrong place at the wrong time?"

"What I think does not matter," replied Davenport. "The police have decided that this is a simple case of theft, *and nothing more.*" He paused and looked over his thick-rimmed glasses at Colophon and Julian. "However, perhaps it would be best not to discuss the key with anyone else until the appropriate time. You never know who may be listening."

Trigue James sat on a bench across the lake at the Lido and watched the entire scene unfold. Davies wouldn't squeal—James was sure of that. He was a professional. He was willing to spend a few months in jail to preserve his reputation, such as it was. It was simply part of doing business. It didn't matter anyway. The only bit of information that Davies had was a cell phone number. A cell phone, by the way, that would soon be at the bottom of the London sewer system.

As far as James was concerned, the game had played itself out. He didn't take unnecessary risks for the sake of any client, and this situation had suddenly become far too risky. The smoke bomb in the bank had been enough of a risk—a highly calculated risk, but a risk nonetheless.

Don't become so confident in your own abilities, James reminded himself, *that you start thinking you can't make a mistake.*

This was James's mantra. He knew he wasn't perfect, and there was always the possibility that he had left some clue behind.

James would leave soon to take a ferry to Calais and then on to Paris and then on to South America. He intended to be as far away from London as possible within the next twenty-four hours. If Treemont wanted that key, he would have to get it himself.

CHAPTER THIRTY-THREE
Regard Him Well

Peachtree Street
Atlanta, Georgia
Monday, December 22
11:35 a.m.

Mull Letterford turned and looked at his son, who stood next to him on the sidewalk. Case, Mull realized with somewhat of a shock, was now taller than he was. And he was handsome. Far more handsome, Mull noted with some pride, than Mull had ever been or could ever hope to be. Case, forgoing his regular attire of raggedy khakis, faded T-shirts, and sandals, had surprised his father that morning by appearing at breakfast in a coat and tie. His normally unruly blond hair was neatly combed back away from his face. For the first time since his son was born, Mull could see in him the future of Letterford & Sons.

"Dad!" Case whispered. "You're staring at me! It's embarrassing."

"Oh, sorry about that," replied Mull Letterford. "Your tie's a bit crooked. Let me straighten it."

Mull reached over and straightened his son's tie. When he finished, he lightly patted his son on his cheek.

"Ready?" Mull asked.

"Ready," Case replied.

"OK, here's the plan. Natasha Limekicker is checked into her hotel under an assumed name. I told her that it was handled this way to protect her from adoring fans. No one knows she is here except me and you. We are meeting her in the coffee shop across the street from the hotel. If all goes well, we can be finished by noon."

"Do you think she has seen the video?" asked Case.

"Who hasn't?" answered Mull, who by this point was well acquainted with the video's worldwide fame.

"Will it matter to her?"

"I don't know," Mull replied. "But there's only one way to find out." He looked up and down Peachtree Street.

"What are you looking for?" Case asked.

"Dogs," Mull replied with a grin.

"Let's get over to the coffee shop before you get arrested for bad jokes." Case grabbed his father's arm and headed across the street.

Mull and Case entered the Steamer Café and Coffee House and proceeded to a table in the back, at which a middle-aged lady with sandy blond hair sipped coffee. Next to her sat a rather dour-looking gentleman in a dark suit.

"Natasha!" Mull said as he approached the table.

"Mull, how good to see you again. Do you remember my agent, Morgan Toombs?"

"Good to see you again," Mull said as he extended his hand to Toombs. Case noticed that Mr. Toombs seemed less than enthusiastic to be meeting with his father. And judging from his father's body language, he clearly had not expected an agent to be present.

"This is my son, Case," Mull said. "I hope you don't mind if he joins us."

"No, not at all," replied Natasha. "Please, have a seat."

Mull and Case sat down at the table. Mull folded his arms and looked across at Natasha Limekicker and her agent. However, before he could utter a single word, the agent spoke.

"Quite an incident in New York," Toombs said.

"Yes," replied Mull. "Well, it's quite the story. You see, we — "

"No explanation is really necessary," interrupted Toombs.

"I see," Mull said.

"My client," Toombs continued, "has a certain, shall we say, expectation of her publisher."

Mull looked at Natasha Limekicker. "Is that so?" Mull asked. Natasha Limekicker did not return his gaze.

"And," the agent continued, "those expectations include not showing up on a video on YouTube covered in mud and being chased by a pack of dogs through the streets of New York."

Mull looked again at Natasha Limekicker, who kept her gaze firmly fixed on her coffee.

"And," the agent continued, "those expectations

also include not showing up on the front page of the 'Living' section of the *Atlanta Journal-Constitution* under the caption 'Publishing Is for the Dogs.'"

Toombs handed a copy of the morning paper to Mull. Neither he nor Case had seen the article or the accompanying photo.

"I can explain," Mull said.

"As I said," Toombs repeated, "no explanation is necessary."

Toombs took a final sip of his coffee and then stood up.

"Thank you for your time this morning," Toombs said. "Natasha, shall we go?"

Mull Letterford looked over at Natasha Lime-kicker one last time.

"I'm sorry," she said. And then she stood and left.

Mull sat back in his chair. He did not appear angry or upset.

"Dad? Are you OK?"

"Tonight's *Monday Night Football*," Mull replied. "How about we grab a pizza and watch the game? Just the guys."

Case looked at his dad. He did not appear delirious, upset, or mad. In fact, he seemed perfectly at ease with what had just occurred. Case grinned. "Yeah, a football game and a pizza would be great."

Chapter Thirty-Four

> "Come, gaoler, bring me where the goldsmith is:
> I long to know the truth hereof at large."

— William Shakespeare, *The Comedy of Errors*

The Grand Library
London
Wednesday, December 24
8:30 p.m.

Treemont stood by the fireplace with his back to the fire. The other members of the family—with the exception of Mull Letterford—were scattered around the room. It was silent except for the pop and crackle of the logs in the fireplace. Although the house was filled with the scents of fresh pine and mulled wine, it held none of the sensed joy and wonder that normally accompanied Christmas Eve. Expectation and anxiety filled the room.

The large oak doors of the library opened suddenly, and Mull Letterford entered, accompanied by his wife, Meg, and son, Case. Audrey Letterford, Mull's sister, followed close behind and closed the doors behind her. Mull stepped to the middle of the room and faced Treemont.

"I was afraid you wouldn't show up," Treemont said in a low voice.

"Then you don't know me very well, do you?" Mull replied.

Uncle Portis walked over to Mull. "Are you prepared to report to the family?"

Mull nodded. Standing straight, he turned and faced the room.

"I failed," he said. He offered no excuses and no explanations for the series of events that had led to this moment.

"So, it is done," said Treemont. "The family must now vote."

Case stood by his father, his eyes red. Mull placed

his arm around his son's shoulder. Meg Letterford grasped her husband's hand.

"No, it's not over."

It was Colophon who spoke. Unbeknownst to the group collected in the library, Colophon had entered the room through the rear door, accompanied by Julian. Colophon walked over to her parents.

"Coly," said Meg Letterford. "Your father has done everything he can."

"But Mom, it's not over," repeated Colophon.

"Dear—" started Mull.

"What about the family treasure? I know where it is! I found it!" exclaimed Colophon.

Treemont laughed. "The family treasure? The family treasure? Are you delusional, girl? *It does not exist!* It is a myth perpetrated by men such as Julian, who have little else to do with their time than chase such fancies."

Mull glared at Treemont. "Do not speak to my daughter in that manner."

"I am tired of delays," replied Treemont. "As the new head of Letterford and—"

Mull interrupted, "You may be the head of the company in a few hours, but for now I remain in charge. You will wait."

Treemont glared at Mull. "You are correct, of course. Enjoy your last taste of ownership." Treemont sat down in one of the large leather club chairs.

Mull turned to his daughter. "Now, what were you saying about the treasure?"

Colophon paused momentarily to collect herself. She looked at her father. He seemed so tired. "As I was saying," she continued, "there is a family treasure. And as some members of our family have long believed, the painting of Miles Letterford was the key to it." Colophon held up the gold key for everyone to see. For the next several minutes, she explained in great detail how she had discovered the clues in the painting, how she and Julian had made their way to Stratford-upon-Avon and barely escaped with their lives, and how they had unlocked the secrets of the tellurion.

"Remarkable!" exclaimed Uncle Portis. "Simply remarkable." Similar comments followed from other members of the family, with the exception, of course, of Treemont.

"So," Audrey Letterford asked, "don't leave us hanging. What does the key unlock?"

"That's where we hit a snag," Colophon responded. "Luckily, Julian was there to help."

Colophon believed that Julian was actually blushing, although it was difficult to tell beneath the five-day-old stubble.

"Well, of course, most of the credit goes to Colophon," Julian stammered. "Brilliant girl, you know."

"Quite," said Mull Letterford.

"I don't mean to be rude," interrupted Uncle Portis, "but what about the key?"

"Oh, of course," replied Julian, who then proceeded to explain how the key had led them to B&C Bank of London.

"And so," asked Mull Letterford, "at the risk of repeating my sister—what does the key unlock?"

Colophon and Cousin Julian looked at each other.

"We don't know," Colophon said. "The bank would not let us have access. Only the owner of Letterford and Sons is permitted to use the key. But we know the key unlocks something special—the treasure."

Treemont laughed. "Four hundred years ago something was left with a goldsmith, who later became a bank? Surely you're not serious! You can't reasonably expect something to still be there?"

"Actually," replied Julian, "she's quite serious. B and C Bank has been the custodian of many important records, documents, jewelry, and other items for hundreds of years. They have the box that this key unlocks. It is quite real."

"However, you have no idea what is in the box?" Treemont asked.

"We don't know," responded Colophon.

"Not a clue," said Julian.

A look of satisfaction crossed Treemont's face. "Tell you what. I'll be owner of this company in, say, a little over three hours. I'll check on the 'treasure' and let you know what it is. Now then, I suppose we should move along to—"

Colophon cleared her throat.

Treemont looked at Colophon with an annoyed expression. "As I was saying—"

Colophon cleared her throat again.

"Yes?" Treemont asked, as he looked down impatiently at Colophon over his glasses.

Colophon walked over to the entrance to the library and opened one of the large oak doors. Walter Davenport entered the room. In his arms, he carried a wooden box.

"Ladies and gentlemen," Colophon said, "please allow me to introduce you to Walter Davenport."

Davenport nodded politely in the direction of the group.

"Mr. Davenport," Julian said, "is a representative from B and C Bank, which has graciously allowed him to come here this evening with Miles Letterford's secure box."

Davenport placed the box on a low table in the middle of the room for everyone to see. It was approximately three feet long by two feet wide and was constructed of a dark, almost black wood edged at its corners with inlaid brass. Carved into the top of the box was the Letterford crest. On the front of the box was a large brass oval inscribed with the symbol for the Greek letter sigma, Σ, identical to the symbol on the key in Mull's office.

"The box is opened by two keys," Davenport explained. "One key is held by the box owner, the second by the bank. As you might expect, it took quite a while for us to locate the bank's key—after all, it has been four hundred years or so since it was last used."

Davenport turned to Mull Letterford.

"Mr. Letterford, I presume."

"Yes," replied Mull.

"And, I believe, you are the current owner of Letterford and Sons."

"Yes, at least as of right now."

"Well, sir, right now is all that matters," replied Davenport.

Davenport pulled a single gold key from his pocket, placed it into one of two slots on the front of the box, and gave it a half turn to the right. There was a click from inside the box. Colophon handed the key to her father, who stepped forward, inserted the second key, and gave it a half turn. There was another click. Mull took a deep breath and then lifted the lid of the box. Everyone in the room gathered behind Mull and Colophon to look.

Inside the box, on a velvet cloth, sat a small greenish-brown container made of glass with a black metal cap.

Treemont reached into the box and pulled out the small container for all to see. "An inkwell! The treasure is an inkwell!"

He laughed. "The treasure is nothing more than an old piece of glass — a personal memento from our esteemed founder." His voice cackled with delight.

Colophon was crestfallen. Her father pulled her close and whispered in her ear. "I am so proud of you."

Treemont's deep voice filled the room. "Shall we move on, or does the girl have any more surprises for us?"

"No," replied Colophon. She couldn't believe it was over. After everything she had been through with Julian, it all amounted to *nothing*.

"Then," continued Treemont, his voice rising in anticipation, "let us move forward with—"

"Actually," Uncle Portis interrupted, "there is more."

Everyone in the room turned toward Uncle Portis, who stood over the box. "Seems like an awful big box for only one small piece of glass, wouldn't you agree?"

He pushed down on the back corners of the velvet cloth on which the inkwell previously sat. The cloth and the board to which it was attached flipped up to reveal a hidden interior. Uncle Portis reached down and pulled out a large brown object and handed it to Mull.

"It's a leather portfolio," said Mull.

"A dried-out leather portfolio!" exclaimed Treemont mockingly. "This has become a farce—a centuries-old joke by our esteemed founder. Now we have paper to go with our dried-up ink! Anything else in that box, Portis? Perhaps Miles's old grocery list?"

Portis held up a piece of paper. "Actually, there is one last thing—a note to our esteemed founder, Miles Letterford."

"From whom? His dry cleaner?" asked Treemont, his voice dripping with sarcasm.

"No," replied Uncle Portis curtly, "from William Shakespeare."

Whatever conversations, noise, or movement that may have otherwise been taking place in the library came to an immediate halt. The fire crackled and popped.

Treemont's eyes went wide. "Shakespeare?" There was, for the first time that evening, a hint of uncertainty in his voice.

"Quite," replied Uncle Portis. "It appears that the Bard once gave Miles a gift of sorts. And based on the contents of this note, I would suggest that this gift was a remarkable treasure indeed."

Mull Letterford, who had been quickly scanning the portfolio, seemed stunned by its contents. "A wonderful treasure indeed," he murmured.

"Well," one of the family members in attendance demanded, "don't keep us in suspense. What is it?"

"As you know," Mull said, "no one has ever found a single play, page, or scribble from any of Shakespeare's works in his own handwriting. This, of course, led to much speculation that the plays were either ghostwritten or that Shakespeare never existed. Such speculation has been the inspiration for dozens of books and articles."

Mull held up the thick leather portfolio for everyone to see.

"This," he continued, his voice growing more confident with each word, "puts all that speculation to rest. What I hold in my hand is nothing less than the original manuscript for *Hamlet,* written in the Bard's own hand, with his edits and stage directions!"

There was a collective gasp among those in the room.

"And there's more," Mull said. "The portfolio also includes a short collection of sonnets and two more plays by Shakespeare—all in his hand."

"Amazing!"

"Remarkable!"

"Outstanding!"

Congratulations filled the air for Colophon, Julian, and their investigatory efforts. Under the din, the library clock softly chimed nine o'clock.

"A treasure beyond treasures!" exclaimed Mull Letterford. "Cowell must be turning in his grave! Can you imagine how excited the scholarly community will be about this?"

Everyone had briefly forgotten about Treemont. Treemont, however, quickly corrected that oversight.

"Congratulations are indeed in order for young Miss Letterford," he said as he moved to the center of the room and started clapping. "This is a great treasure indeed! And, as the new owner of Letterford and

Sons, I promise to take great care of this valuable piece of family history. Now, I don't mean to undermine this grand achievement or otherwise disrupt this festive atmosphere. However, I presume we are now ready to formalize my standing as the new owner of Letterford. I assume we all agree that Mull has not met the terms of our agreement. Does anyone disagree?"

Treemont looked around as one head after another nodded, albeit reluctantly, in agreement.

Treemont then turned to Mull.

"I assume you are a man of your word?" Treemont asked.

"I am," Mull replied.

"Dear?"

Mull looked around. It was his wife, Meg, who had called to him.

"Yes?" Mull replied.

"I have something to say," Meg Letterford said. She was holding the portfolio, and there was a decidedly businesslike tone to her voice.

"Say anything you please," Mull replied.

Treemont started to protest, but Meg Letterford cut him short with a quick glance over the top of her glasses — a skill she had perfected from years in the classroom.

"I believe," Meg said, "that the terms of the agreement have, in fact, been satisfied in full."

"What do you mean?" demanded Treemont. "Mull did not meet the demands of the family by the deadline. He was required to provide at least three new works by a best-selling author. He failed. There is nothing more to discuss."

Meg Letterford held up the portfolio for all to see. Colophon, who had dropped deep into the crevices of one of the great leather chairs, shot up immediately.

"You would concede," asked Meg, "that Shakespeare is a best-selling author—at least posthumously?"

"Of course," replied Treemont.

Meg Letterford smiled. "Scholars have long wondered why Shakespeare simply quit writing after he returned to Stratford from London. Some scholars have speculated that he did not stop writing. Rather, they speculate that due to his political and religious leanings, he was forced out of London and into seclusion—but that he kept writing. It now appears that they were correct. *Hamlet,* of course, is one of the most recognized plays ever written. However, I did not recognize the sonnets and the other plays included in the portfolio—and for good reason: they have never been published or distributed in any form. You have your three new works, previously unpublished and written by perhaps the greatest writer in history. The agreement has been satisfied."

"But, wait . . ." stammered Treemont. "That's not the agreement."

Uncle Portis's response was curt and to the point: "That *was* the agreement—three new works by a best-selling author. And they are the exclusive property of Letterford and Sons. Mull Letterford has satisfied the agreement in full, and the business is his to run."

Portis turned and looked at the rest of the family. "Are we all in agreement?"

Everyone in the room nodded and shouted in accordance, with the exception, of course, of Treemont.

"Then it is concluded," Uncle Portis said.

And the fireplace cracked and popped. And the room was filled with the scent of fresh pine and mulled wine.

Treemont slipped quietly out of the library and walked to the entrance hall of the Letterford home. He pulled on his overcoat and glanced outside to make sure his cab had arrived. He then looked back down the entrance hall to ensure that he was alone. No one was there. He pulled out his cell phone and placed a call.

"It didn't go exactly according to plan," he said. "But I found what I needed—they have the box. It had an inkwell. *Nothing* else important was in it."

There was a pause as someone on the other end of the phone spoke.

"No," Treemont replied, "they have no idea."

Another pause.

"We have work to do," he said. "It's now within reach."

Another pause.

"Yes," he said. "You're right. It could not have worked out better. I will see you in Boston in a week."

Treemont ended the call and placed the cell phone in his breast pocket.

Case peeked through the window in the entrance hall and watched Treemont step into the back seat of a waiting cab.

Had Treemont really just said that there was nothing else important in the box? How could he say that? Hadn't he seen what they had found?

Case had noticed Treemont sneak out of the library. And he had noticed something else, too—that Treemont, for all the fuss and fury he had exhibited, did not seem particularly upset as he slipped away. In fact, Treemont had seemed almost, well, smug.

This had bothered Case, and he had decided to follow Treemont. Case had exited through the back of the library and had made his way to the front of the house. Standing just outside the entrance hall and out of view, Case had overheard Treemont engaged in a conversation with someone on the phone.

And it was that conversation that now concerned Case. He needed to talk to Colophon.

Case walked back down the hallway and around the stairs and stood at the back entrance to the library. Across the room he could see his father, his sister, and his mother.

They were happy.

The stress and worry that had weighed so heavily on his father for the last several months had disappeared in an instant.

Maybe I didn't hear what I thought I heard.

Case watched as his father grabbed Colophon by her hands and twirled her in a swooping circle. Colophon squealed with delight.

Case made up his mind. Whatever he heard—or thought he heard—could wait. Tonight was not the right time.

Case crossed the room and joined the family in celebration.

Epilogue

The small parcel from Julian was postmarked Abergavenny, Wales. Inside, Colophon discovered a single handwritten page.

> Colophon:
>   There is no time for small talk. In our quest, we followed one clue to another, which led us to the Shakespeare manuscripts. We all assumed the manuscripts were, in fact, Miles Letterford's great treasure.
>   We were wrong.
>   The manuscripts were simply another clue.
>   I will write further.
>   Julian

FINI

Appendix

Author's note: The chapter titles are derived from different plays and sonnets by William Shakespeare.

Chapter 1: What News, I Prithee?
   King Henry VI, Part II, act 3, scene 2
Chapter 2: Homeward Did They Bend Their Course
   The Comedy of Errors, act 1, scene 1
Chapter 3: My Books . . . Shall Be My Company
   The Taming of the Shrew, act 1, scene 1
Chapter 4: The Ill Wind Which Blows
   King Henry IV, Part II, act 5, scene 3
Chapter 5: Under Thy Own Life's Key
   All's Well That Ends Well, act 1, scene 1
Chapter 6: Be Bounteous at Our Meal
   Antony and Cleopatra, act 4, scene 2
Chapter 7: To Me Thy Secrets Tell
   The Winter's Tale, act 4, scene 3
Chapter 8: To Desperate Ventures
   King Richard III, act 5, scene 3

— COLOPHON —

THUS ENDS THIS BOOK:
A Tale of the Letterford Family
BY DERON R. HICKS.

✢

PRINTED BY HOUGHTON MIFFLIN HARCOURT,
AND FIRST OFFERED TO THE DISCERNING PUBLIC
ON THE FOURTH DAY OF SEPTEMBER, MMXII.
THE TEXT FONTS ARE NEW CENTURY SCHOOLBOOK, EUPHORIGENIC, AND CAPTAIN KIDD.

—— ✢ ——

with great thanks & appreciation to the following:

AGENT: STEVEN CHUDNEY
PUBLISHER: BETSY GROBAN
EDITORIAL DIRECTOR: MARY WILCOX
EDITOR: ANN RIDER
EDITORIAL INTERN: AMY CHERRIX
MANAGING EDITOR: ANN-MARIE PUCILLO
COPYEDITORS: JANET BIEHL AND ALISON KERR MILLER
PROOFREADER: SARAH CHAFFEE PARIS
ART DIRECTOR: CAROL CHU
ASSISTANT DESIGNER: SUSANNA VAGT
PRODUCTION MANAGER: TRISH MCGINLEY
JACKET ILLUSTRATOR: GILBERT FORD
INTERIOR ILLUSTRATOR: MARK EDWARD GEYER
MARKETING MANAGER: LISA DISARRO
PUBLICIST: RACHEL WASDYKE

✢ ✢ ✢

DERON HICKS is the author of the Shakespeare Mysteries series. As an attorney, he investigates mysteries for a living, so it's only natural that he would write one about William Shakespeare, one of literature's most puzzling people. With his own children's natural curiosity as inspiration, Deron set out to reveal a bit of the mystery of the real world and show that many of its secrets (and stories) still wait to be told. He lives in Warm Springs, Georgia.

MARK EDWARD GEYER is best known as the illustrator of two Stephen King novels: *Rose Madder* and *The Green Mile*. Mark comes from a line of French Canadian artists. He lives in Atlanta, Georgia.

TURN THE PAGE FOR A SNEAK PEAK OF

TOWER OF THE FIVE ORDERS

Colophon Letterford has discovered a long-lost family treasure and saved the family business. However, as familiar foes continue to plot and scheme against her family, Colophon and her cousin Julian discover that there may be more to the family treasure than they had ever anticipated. More clues lead to more questions, and Colophon must unravel the secrets of Oxford's Tower of the Five Orders to reveal the true legacy of her ancient ancestor.

COMING IN FALL 2013

Prologue

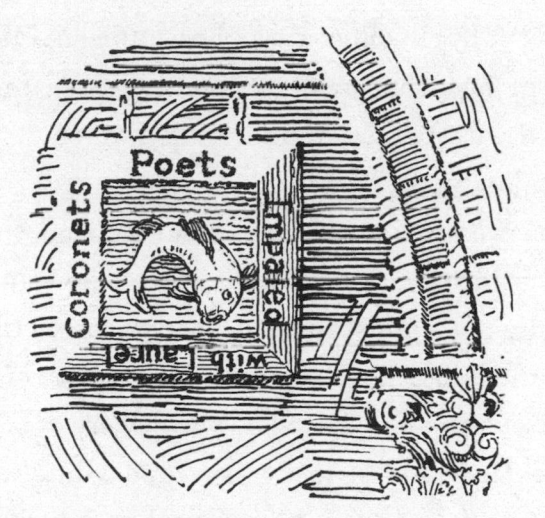

Elanor Bull's Public House
Deptford, England
May 30, 1593

The smell of roasted meat and the noisy clank of kitchen pots filled the room. A young potboy whistled as he gathered dishes from a table and shuffled them off to the back of the house.

Christopher Marlowe gazed out the window at the rapidly fading sunlight. He took a long draw from his tankard of ale, closed his eyes, and savored the brief moment of peace. It had been, to say the least, a bad year. The plague had once again cast a spell of death across London. In an effort to slow its progress, by order of the Crown, the theaters had been closed. As if the loss of his livelihood was not sufficient, Marlowe had—in just the previous month—been arrested, charged with heresy, and forbidden to leave the city until called upon for trial.

Marlowe was not a fool. He knew that the trial would be a mere formality. It was clear that forces were aligned against him—the same forces that had once called upon his assistance. The charge of heresy was utter nonsense. Facts, however, were of no consequence. He would be lucky to escape a date with the executioner's sword. Two days earlier it had seemed all but certain that he would spend the remaining days of his life in shackles and under guard. And yet for some reason, he had been allowed to remain at liberty until the time for his trial.

Odd, Marlowe thought as he took another drink from his tankard. *The Crown is usually not so . . .*

He paused in midthought.

Fie! What a fool I am. Of course they let me go.

He contemplated the obvious: that they had never intended to provide him a trial. He knew far too much—his fate had already been decided.

I shall leave for France forthwith.

Marlowe started to rise from his seat when he noticed that the room had suddenly turned silent. No banging of pots in the kitchen. No scuffing of chairs along the stone floor. No murmur of conversation.

Nothing.

Marlowe peered around the room. It was empty. Elanor Bull, who owned and operated the public house, was nowhere to be seen. The potboy's whistle was silent. Marlowe had been so absorbed in his own thoughts that he had failed to notice what was taking place around him.

Fie again!

He set his tankard on the table, and his hand went instantly to the dagger at his side. The front door creaked open. Marlowe shielded his eyes from the light of the late afternoon sun as it streamed through the open doorway. He could not see who had entered or how many.

When the door shut, a large man dressed in black turned to face him. He held a sword at his side. Two men stood beside the man in black—their swords drawn.

"Robert Poley," said Marlowe to the man standing at the door. "What news? Have ye come on behalf of God, the Crown, or the Devil?"

Poley spoke slowly, his voice deep and raspy.

"Neither God nor the Crown has any use for thee, Christopher Marlowe."

"Aye, 'tis true, Robert Poley," Marlowe replied, "but I suspect that it is on the Devil's behalf that a man such as yourself was sent."

Marlowe held the dagger close to his hip as he stood and moved toward the center of the room. He needed time to assess the situation. "So the Earl of Essex prefers his secrets in the grave?" he said.

Poley grunted and spat on the floor. "Impertinent dog," he growled. "'Tis worms who shall bear witness to what secrets ye hold."

Marlowe knew that there was a rear door leading to a narrow alley behind the tavern. He could make it to the alley before Poley and his men had time to react. But he also knew Poley—he would have the exit covered. The only way out would be through the front door and at the point of his own dagger. Marlowe cursed himself for lack of more substantial arms.

At that moment, Marlowe heard a faint shuffle of feet in the darkness behind him.

He smiled. *Clumsy fool.*

Marlowe pivoted backwards just as a sword thrust at him from the shadows. His dagger flashed from his side and into the right arm of his attacker. The man screamed as the sword fell from his hand and clanked onto the hard stone floor. Marlowe grabbed the sword and turned to face Poley and his henchmen. He grinned as he ran the steel of his dagger down the blade of the sword. "Ye may seek to whet thy swords on my bones," he said, "but ye will find me a most unwilling grindstone."

"So be it," growled Poley.

The clank of steel on steel rang through the room and into the street beyond.

Chapter One

Auspicious

Auspicious—Presenting favorable circumstances
or showing signs of a favorable outcome.

The discovery of the Shakespeare manuscripts by
Colophon Letterford and her cousin Julian did not
go unnoticed. Universally hailed as the most important literary discovery of the last century, if not of all
time, the story seized the public's imagination.

The *New York Times* ran a five-part series about
the discovery. The *Boston Globe* featured a picture
of Mull Letterford, Colophon's father, on the front
page of its Sunday edition. An editorial in *Le Monde*

praised the Letterford family and their contributions to literary history.

Magazines such as *Time, Newsweek, National Geographic,* and *Bon Appétit* profiled the discovery with cover stories.

Mull Letterford was interviewed on NPR, CNN, Fox, CBS, NBC, ABC, the BBC, the CBC, CCTV, and Radio Liechtenstein. Colophon was invited to the set of *MythBusters*—her all-time favorite TV show —and celebrated her thirteenth birthday with the cast and crew. Julian appeared on *Good Morning America.* It was the first time Colophon had ever seen him with his hair combed and his face shaved —and wearing a tie.

The academic community—which could barely contain its collective glee—geared up for what was anticipated to be years of research, examination, interpretation, and explication of the manuscripts. Requests poured in to Letterford & Sons from researchers for opportunities to study the original manuscripts. Every reputable (and not so reputable) Shakespearean scholar on the planet offered his or her services free of charge just for the opportunity to have access to the manuscripts. Preorders for the summer edition of the *Shakespeare Quarterly* overwhelmed the limited staff and resources of the Johns Hopkins University Press. Meg Letterford, Colophon's mother, received invitations from across the academic spectrum to join faculties as a visiting professor. The Folger Shakespeare Library in Washington, D.C., held a symposium that coincided with a week-long exhibit of several of the manuscripts. Tickets for the exhibit sold out in minutes.

Numerous offers were made to purchase the manuscripts, for stunning amounts. But Mull Letterford held firm. The manuscripts, he said repeatedly, belonged to humanity. He could not bear the thought of them ending up in the private collection of some billionaire, never to be studied or enjoyed by the rest of the world.

The Letterford name, well known and respected within literary circles for centuries, had now become well known and respected in the world at large.

It was a glorious time.

And it was short-lived.